Light Riders and the Morenci Mine Murder

A Time Travel Mystery by
Ann I. Goldfarb

Also by this author:

The Face Out Of Time

Ripple Rider: An Anguillan Adventure In Time

The Last Tag

*Light Riders And The
Fleur-de-lis Murder*

*Light Riders And The
Missouri Mud Murder*

**Two
Cats
Press**

Light Riders and the Morenci Mine Murder

Ann I. Goldfarb

*Light Riders and the
Morenci Mine Murder*

Copyright © May 2012 by Ann I. Goldfarb
All Rights Reserved

Published by

 **Two
Cats
Press**

Surprise, Arizona, U.S.A.
Printed in the U.S.A.

ISBN 13: 978-1-937083-24-3
ISBN 10: 10: 1937083241

Library of Congress Card Catalog Number:
LCCN: LCCN 2013946124

This book's interior and cover was designed by Jean Boles:
http://jeanboles.elance.com

For Valentina

With fondest memories and love for you, your family, and our dear friends in Moscow

PART ONE:

Prisms

Excerpt from Aeden's writing journal, sixth grade

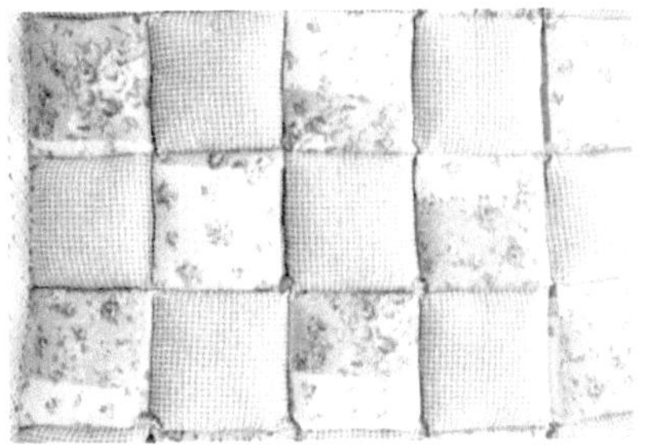

I remember watching my grandmother take the corner of a quilt, and with small pieces of ribbon, mold it into the shape of an animal. Her hands created a soft, cuddly animal that I could press against me during the night because I had forgotten to bring my stuffed bear with me. When I told my brother about this, years later, he had no idea that our grandmother was able to do such a thing.

That's how it is; we see bits and pieces of people, never the full image. Pixels and particles, not the print... So it came as no surprise to me when we had to help our parents clean out great Auntie Zanne's house, that we knew so little about her. We just had the pixels, and they weren't enough.

Aeden

Chapter One:
Aeden

"Face it, Aeden, Auntie Zanne was a hoarder. We'll never get out of here. You can kiss summer in Portland good-bye 'cause we're stuck in Timbukwhat Waddell, Arizona. So much for a family vacation! This is a stinkin' nightmare! See for yourself! Mom and Dad can't even get past the front room!"

I watched as my 13 year old brother wiped some sort of dirt off his hands and onto his t-shirt before heading back into Auntie Zanne's small stucco house. Our great aunt was my grandfather's sister-in-law and the last time we saw her must have been at least five or six years ago on our only trip out west. I was eight or nine at the time and fascinated by the menagerie that made up her surroundings, beginning with the sea of weeds in her yard, old Mexican pottery, bizarre bronze lawn sculptures and water goblets. We never actually went into her house. You could say it was a short visit. This trip was bound to be different. And Ryn's fussing and fuming was going to make it seem longer.

"Well, Aeden, aren't you at least gonna come inside, or are you gonna stand there all day looking at the dead weeds?" Ryn swung the rusty screen door aside and continued his tirade. "Stinkin' nightmare."

I started towards the door.

"It's not her fault she died and we're the only relatives left."

"Yeah, but it's her fault that she had to collect so much crap that they're gonna need to excavate a whole new landfill for it!"

"Will you two stop yelling at each other and come in here to give us a hand!" My father was beginning to get exasperated and it showed in the tone of his voice.

"What do you want us to do, Dad?" I asked as I stepped into a small tiled room with a low ceiling and enough dust to give the entire city of Phoenix one big allergy attack.

"You and Ryn can start in the big bedroom. Clothing that looks halfway decent can go in the boxes for Goodwill, anything else can go in the trash pile by the side of the house."

"Ryn's going to want to throw out everything!"

My father's voice got louder. "That's why both of you are working together. Understand?"

"What's mom doing?"

"Washing and boxing old dishes and glassware."

"No problem. Ryn and I will be fine."

"Thought so." My father's voice trailed off as I stepped over piles of frames, pottery, boxes and cartons that lined both sides of the narrow hallway.

Ryn was already sitting on the bed with his arms crossed when I walked into the room.

"So, what do you say we just open the window and start tossing the stuff on the pile?" he asked.

"I say we do it right. It might be interesting ...I mean, fashions and stuff from all kinds of decades."

"Interesting for you, maybe. Water boarding sounds like more fun if you ask me."

"Well, I'm not asking, Ryn, I just want to get this over with, too."

"Okay, Aeden, I'll start with the dresser over there, that is, if I can crawl over the pile of blankets on the floor."

"Do you have any idea why she lived this way?"

"Beats me. But I'll tell you one thing. If I ever die and leave a mess like this, just set a match to it!"

"Very funny, Ryn. Better hope no one decides to inspect your bedroom!"

I opened the door to a small closet and looked in. The clothes on hangers were packed so tight they probably could have stood up by themselves. With Ryn in the other corner of the room, I decided to start with Auntie Zanne's wardrobe.

For the next half hour, my brother and I only spoke in strings of one or two syllable words, usually preceded by some sort of guttural sound.

"Ugh. Old housedresses."

"Yuch. Yellow nightgowns."

"Ick. Dead animal wraps."

From evening gowns that were probably popular when Mamie Eisenhower was First Lady, to cut off jeans and faded tie dye, Auntie Zanne seemed to have it all in her possession.

"What do you suppose she was like?"

"Who?" Ryn asked.

"Who do you think? Lady Gaga? Auntie Zannie, you idiot. What do you suppose she was like?"

"I dunno. Why are you asking me? I have no idea. I only know the same stuff you do. The stuff mom and dad told us."

"Yeah, and other than the fact that she was some kind of scientist, it wasn't much. Although mom did say that Auntie Zanne was an incredible woman. She was on her own for most of her life and used whatever resources she had to put herself through school. Mom also said that Auntie Zanne was amazingly good looking in her day."

"Too bad she wasn't amazingly neat or we wouldn't have to be going through all of her old crap."

I shrugged and went back to work removing dresses, pants and gowns from the closet. Ryn did salvage a few things but most of the items in the dresser wound up in the pile marked for garbage. My brother kept heaping more stuff on it before letting out a long, torturous sigh.

"I'm taking a break and getting a coke from the cooler. Want anything?"

"Yeah, bring me a diet coke. I could use a break, too, but I just want to finish cleaning out this closet. It's like one of those fun house rooms in Disney World. It looks small but it just keeps growing and growing."

"Tell me about it…"

I could hear Ryn cursing under his breath as he tried not to trip over the stuff in the hallway. The sun had moved to this side of the house and a dusty beam of light illuminated the small closet. Nothing was left hanging. Shoes from the bottom were tossed out, along with some old thread bare sheets that were on the top shelf. I was just about to shut the door when I noticed something odd. The proportions weren't right. The top of the closet should be the same size and dimensions as the rest of it, but it wasn't. I was sure of it.

Quickly, I tossed the pile of "catch-all" stuff that had started to accumulate on a small chair, to the bed and moved the chair beneath the top shelf of the closet. Leaning my weight on the door frame to the closet, I stood up and began to tap on the walls. I was right! One of them was hollow. And it was hollow for a reason.

****

Old crumpled note left in wastebasket from Ryn's seventh grade detention

I'm probably gonna spend the next ten years in psycho-therapy or some sort of therapy 'cause no one in their right mind would ever believe me. Why we had to clean out crazy great Aunt Zanne's house is beyond me. I mean, couldn't my parents have just sold the damn place to begin with? Well, it doesn't matter. I'll have something to tell my new shrink.

Ryn

Chapter Two:
Ryn

Geez, it wasn't bad enough we had to clean out this hornet's nest of a house that great Auntie Zanne left us, but now Aeden goes and decides that maybe there's more stuff behind the walls. Hell! There's enough crap in front of us to wreck this summer and maybe even the next one! We didn't need to go looking for more. So when I came back into the room with her can of diet coke, I couldn't help but freak.

"What the heck are you doing? If you fall and break your neck, mom and dad are probably gonna blame me!"

"I think there's something behind this wall, Ryn. Give me a hand."

"Oh, like there's not enough junk in front of your eyes? You have to go looking for it?"

"I mean it, Ryn; the space has been hollowed out. See for yourself. I just can't seem to find a way to open it up without breaking through the wall itself."

"Get down from there and I'll take a look."

Still facing the closet, Aeden jumped down, letting go of the door frame at the last second.

"See for yourself. On the left hand side."

I handed her the coke and climbed up before speaking.

"You know, if we do open up whatever's in here, we could be letting in bats, or scorpions or who knows what!"

"Since when are you afraid of that stuff?"

"Since I don't want to spend the rest of my vacation, or whatever you call this, in an emergency room."

"Come on, Ryn; just take a look like you said you would!"

Aeden was right. The wall was hollowed out. But it didn't need a hammer to break it apart. In the lower left hand corner was some sort of small latch. I moved my hand further up and felt a similar one on the top. Easy latch. Homemade. With a quick twist, I moved the small pieces of metal just enough to see the wall move forward.

"Aeden, grab me a clothes hanger!"

Bending the tip of the hanger, I made a hook that was just narrow enough to wedge behind the wall and give it a pull.

"Look out, Aeden! If a million bats come flying out, don't say I didn't warn you!"

But no bats came out. No scorpions either. Just enough dust to make me sneeze and wish I never agreed to do this. But once the wall opened, I was curious, too.

"What the hell," I muttered to myself as I leaned into the closet and reached my hand into the space. Immediately, I felt something. A box. Some sort of box.

"What do you see? Did you find anything?"

"It's a box, Aeden, a large box. Hold your horses, I'm gonna pull it forward and hope it doesn't fall."

The box was about the size of a small printer or maybe one of those crate things you see teachers carrying their supplies in, but it wasn't heavy. I shoved it forward until I could grab it on both ends. Then I turned around slowly and handed it to Aeden before getting off of the chair.

The box was a plain cardboard box, sealed with clear mailing tape. But one glance at the writing on top and I swear I felt every hair on the back of my head stand up. Aeden gasped and stood there, mouth wide open, eyes, too.

In large magic marker ink, the words stood out like an advertisement. Only it wasn't. It was an invitation and it had been sitting for years.

TO: AEDEN AND RYN
WITH LOVE, AUNTIE ZANNE
(FOR YOUR EYES <u>ONLY</u>)

Chapter Three:
Aeden

Ryn glared at me before turning his attention to the cardboard box.

"Are you going to stand there staring at that thing all day or are you going to open it?"

"Don't you think we should tell Mom and Dad?"

"Didn't you read what it said, Aeden? It said *For Your Eyes Only*. Maybe she didn't want Mom and Dad to see what's in there."

"Why? What could possibly be in here that she didn't want them to see?"

"Gee, Aeden, I don't know. But I'm not about to stand here all day playing *Twenty-one Guesses* with you when we could just open the darn thing and see for ourselves!"

Then, Ryn did exactly that. He ripped the brittle masking tape from the sides and removed the lid. Before I could get a good look, he spoke.

"Just looks like a pile of notes and some prisms to me."

"Prisms?"

By now, I was looking at the box and none of its contents made sense to me. I watched as Ryn held up prisms of varying sizes.

"What do you suppose she wanted us to do with prisms? Build a chandelier?"

I reached in and removed a yellowing pile of notes that were clipped together with an old metal paperclip. The rust had bled onto the paper.

"I think she meant for us to read these notes, Ryn, not just grab the stuff and see what we can do with it. It's not like one of your bikes or remote control cars where you can just figure it out. This time you'll have to play by the rules."

"You're just jealous, Aeden. Always have been. Just because you need to read the manuals for stuff from cover to cover before putting anything together doesn't mean the rest of us do."

"I think in this case, it does. Because you don't know what Auntie Zanne intended us to do with the prisms."

"Whoa. Don't get all crazy, Aeden. They're just prisms."

"Then why did she write *For Your Eyes Only?* Huh?"

My fingers tried to separate the notes but the corners of the papers kept crumbling. Finally, I found a clear space on one of the dressers and set the notes down so that I could read them without having them disintegrate. But what I read made no sense, and when I read them out loud they made even less sense.

IT WAS ALWAYS IN THE REFRACTION.

REFRACTED LIGHT IS TIME ITSELF.

TIME IS CONSTANT. MOVE WITH IT AND MEET DEATH AT THE END. MOVE THROUGH IT AND THERE IS NO END.

"Is she saying there's such a thing as time travel?"

"Come on Aeden, what she's really saying is *take me to the looney bin.* Okay. So now we know for sure. Auntie Zanne was nuts. Certifiable. Not just a hoarder, but a downright nut case. Just toss the box with the rest of the stuff, Aeden."

"I'm not tossing anything, Ryn. Not until I read everything in her notes."

"You mean there's more?"

"Yeah, there's lots more, plus some sort of small envelope that got wedged between the sheets of paper."

I removed it carefully and looked at the front. There was only one word on it—Ryn.

"Well, go ahead. Open it. It's yours."

Ryn gave me one of his "I can't believe I'm doing this" looks before tearing open the envelope.

"Well, what's in it? What does she say?"

Ryn stared at a piece of paper without realizing he had dropped something.

"This can't be for me. I have no idea what she's talking about."

I started to raise my voice.

"What does it say?"

"It says '*He's sorry for not telling you the truth. Hope you forgive him.*' Now what on earth is that supposed to mean?"

"Maybe it was meant for a different Ryn. Maybe there's another Ryn in our family."

"I don't think so, Aeden. Remember what mom and dad told us about our names? I was supposed to be Ryan but they forgot the "a" on my birth certificate so they just kept Ryn. Then, when you were born a year later, they wanted to name you Eden for the Garden of Eden, but put the missing "a" from my name on the front of yours."

I took a breath and realized he was right. He was the only Ryn. Then what did Auntie Zanne mean?

Before I could say anything, Ryn looked down and realized that something had fallen to the floor. It was a clipping from an old newspaper. And I could tell that something was wrong the minute he picked it up.

"I don't believe this. It's not possible. It's just…"

"What is it? Show me, Ryn."

"It's an old black and white photo from some newspaper. They cut off the heading on the top but someone wrote a date on the side."

"So what's so odd about that?"

Ryn's voice started to get louder and faster.

"What's so odd about that? What's so freaking odd? I'll tell you what's odd, Aeden…"

Then, he slowed down, speaking each word as if it were his last.

"The photo is a picture of me."

Chapter Four:

Ryn

*T*he date said *July 1930* and sure enough, it was me. I was leaning forward, out the window of a train, my hands clenched on the ledge, with a few boys on either side of me. I was trying to take a closer look at the photo when Aeden snatched it from my hand and began to freak out.

"Oh my gosh, oh my gosh, OH MY GOSH. You got back in time, Ryn. That's what Auntie Zanne is trying to tell us. There's a way to get back in time and it has something to do with these prisms. What did that note say? Something about refracted light?"

"Aeden, refracted light is just light whose path has been bent. Don't they teach you anything in science? Light changes speed as it moves from one place to the next, and when it does, it bends."

"But maybe Auntie Zanne found a way to move with the light. You know, move through time. That's probably why she left us the prisms. To move through time! Look, you must have done it once or you wouldn't be in that picture. And she left this stuff so you could go back and maybe find out why some guy lied to you."

"You read too many fantasy books, Aeden. And people lie all the time. There's a logical explanation for the picture and the note. We just don't know what it is."

I was about to take another look at the prisms when I heard my father's voice.

"Ryn and Aeden, we're going to grab a bite to eat in a few minutes so finish up the packing. Mom and I are getting hungry and you two must be starving."

The truth of the matter was that my sister and I were so rattled by the note and photo that we hadn't even thought of eating. Still, we couldn't let our parents know what we had discovered.

"Okay, Dad. Aeden and I will be right out!"

The box was still on the corner of the bed where Aeden and I left it. Quickly, I threw the photo into it along with the notes that were on the dresser. Then I set it on the floor and covered it up with a few old blankets. Aeden watched my every move before she spoke.

"Think it'll be safe there?"

"Who's gonna take it, Aeden? 1-800-Hoarding?"

Just then I heard my father bellowing.

"We're leaving now! Ryn and Aeden! Hurry up!"

But Aeden didn't hurry. She insisted on moving that stupid box back to the closet.

"Just leave it on the floor of the closet, Okay?" I was beginning to lose my temper with her. Guess seeing yourself in a photograph taken years before you were born will do that to you. "The box will be fine. FINE! Come on! Mom and Dad are waiting and you don't want them snooping around in here!"

Aeden nodded.

"There was another piece of paper, Ryn. But I didn't think it mattered. It's still in the box."

"What did it say?"

"I don't know. I mean, I don't understand it. It was just some sort of a scribbling or maybe a formula. You know, like for the area of a circle or the perimeter of something."

"Do you remember what it said exactly? Oh, never mind!"

I threw the lid off the box and looked for myself. Sure enough there was a yellowing piece of paper with the formula *n1.sin 01 = n2.sin02* scrawled across it. A small footnote was beneath it:

Use the prisms so there are no boundaries for light. It will keep going and so will you.

Yep. Great Auntie Zanne was nuts all right. But I had Aeden take a pen from her bag and write down the original formula. I figured that when we got back to our motel that night, I'd Google whatever it was she had written. Auntie Zanne may have lived in no-mans-land but at least the motel was in Phoenix, complete with WIFI and cable.

Chapter Five:
Aeden

"How much longer do we have to keep torturing ourselves at Auntie Zanne's house?" Ryn asked as he stuffed himself with a fourth piece of pizza.

I could see by the look on my parents' faces that they kind of agreed with him but couldn't do much about it. My mom glanced at my dad, took a sip of her iced tea and spoke.

"At the rate we're going, we'll have the house ready for the estate people by the end of the week."

Ryn groaned. "Three more days of this? Three more days?"

My mother continued.

"The house will be put up for auction and the usable contents sold at an estate sale. But if we don't clear it out and clean it out, it will be difficult to sell."

Ryn grabbed his chest, faking a heart attack.

"Clean it out? You mean we have to clean the place as well? There are laws against child labor!"

"Ryn's right, Mom. This is really unfair. It's the worst summer we've ever had."

Then my father added his two cents.

"This is no picnic for your mother and me either, but it's an obligation we have. Besides, there's a possibility we may get the proceeds from the sale. Proceeds that would go towards your college funds."

So what could Ryn and I say without sounding like spoiled brats? I took my chances anyway.

"What did you mean when you said '*may get the proceeds*'? Who else would get them?"

My dad leaned into the table and took a breath, a signal that a long explanation would be coming.

"Actually, that brings up something that your mom and I wanted to talk with you about. Tomorrow we need to meet with the bank that holds your great aunt's trust. Without it, the state would be in charge of her estate. Thankfully she had the good sense to set up a trust. So...with mom and me at the bank in

Phoenix for most of the morning, both of you can either work at the house or sit in the lobby of the bank and wait until our meeting is over. The choice is yours."

Ryn grimaced.

"What about staying at the motel? Aeden and I will be fine."

"Your father and I are not comfortable with that. Phoenix is a big city with big city crime. You're much safer at the house in Waddell or with us at the bank. No other options. Understood?"

Before I could say a word, Ryn spoke for us.

"We'll go the house. At least we'll have something to do."

"Yeah, Ryn's right. I'm sure there are lots of boxes that need to be cleaned out, even if it takes light years!"

I felt the quick jab of Ryn's elbow before I could say anything else, but my foot was fast and I managed to nail his ankle just as our parents got up and walked to the counter to pay the bill.

"What the hell did you kick me for?"

"'Cause you elbowed me!"

"You were about to go yammering about the prisms and light, and all the weird time travel stuff. Listen, Aeden, we'll check out that formula on the motel's computer tonight, and tomorrow when we're by ourselves at the house, we'll figure out what to do with the prisms."

"You mean you believe Auntie Zanne may have had a way to move through time?"

"Not exactly. But she may have figured out how to bend it."

The rest of the afternoon as we were forced to lug boxes from the kitchen to the outside "staging area" as my mom liked to call it, all I could think about was what Ryn said. I mean, if anyone in our family understood scientific stuff, it was Ryn. I think that's because he took great pleasure in taking things apart and putting them back together. Yeah, there were a few casualties along the way, like our dad's wristwatch and a knife sharpener that could now break metal, but still...Ryn was pretty smart when it came to that stuff. So I figured he must be on to something and maybe that formula made sense to him 'cause it sure didn't to me.

"Mom and Dad can't hear us, Ryn," I whispered as I handed him a box of silverware to add to the growing pile that had started to take over the yard. "What did you mean about bending time?"

"I don't know, Aeden, but that formula looked somewhat familiar. I won't know until tonight when we can use the computer at the motel. I swear, as soon as I'm old enough to start earning some money, I'm buying myself a MacBook Air!"

"By that time they'll have invented something else."

"Who cares? I just need my own computer. We live like barbarians! Only one computer in our house and that's what? Like eight years old already?"

"Forget about our computer, why would that formula look familiar?"

"Because I think I might have used it once. I just can't seem to remember."

Chapter Six:
Ryn

*I*t was really weird, but every time I thought about that formula I felt as if I was getting closer to something that keeps moving further away. You know, like trying to remember a really cool dream first thing in the morning only to have it get fuzzier by the time you get out of bed. Aeden wasn't much help either. She just kept nagging and nagging me, even as I tried to Google the formula later that night.

"Well, what does it say? What sites are you going to?"

"Give me a minute, Aeden. There's like a million of these physics sites!"

It seemed like every university on the planet had its own take on the formula, but they all knew what it was, and I should've, too, if I had remembered the program at the "Oregon Museum of Science and Industry" that our eighth grade class went to in the fall. No wonder the formula sounded familiar. It was! I looked at my sister and pointed to the screen on the computer.

"Aeden, this is a formula for refraction and it's a famous one—*Snell's Law*."

"What does it mean?"

"A bunch of stuff, really. It's about light being able to go full speed in a vacuum but slower elsewhere."

"Is there more?"

"Oh yeah. Light is only refracted or bent when it hits something. But if it doesn't hit anything then it keeps on going."

"So what does that have to do with time travel?"

"I have no idea, but apparently our crazy Aunt Zanne did. That's why she mentioned the prisms. I think she found a way to set up the prisms and use that light to move through time. Or, at least that's what her bizarre little notes say."

"I think you found a way, too, Ryn, or you wouldn't have been in that picture."

I tried not to think about it, but I couldn't ignore the facts. I really was in a picture from 1930 and I had no idea how I got there. But one thing was certain. I was going to find out. Aeden and I would have the house to ourselves the next morning and I planned to find out everything I could about prisms and light before then. But what I didn't find out was why the note said that some guy was sorry he lied. Lied about what? What the heck did he do? And more important, where the hell was I?

"Okay, Aeden," I said. "Here's the deal. First thing tomorrow when we get dropped off at the house, we take that box of prisms and re-read Auntie Zanne's notes. If I'm guessing correctly, there's a specific way that we need to set up the prisms and then step inside while the light moves from surface to surface."

"Then what?"

"Then we hold our breath and wait for the ride of our lives!"

"You're serious?"

"Well, I'm in the picture, aren't I?"

"But what about me, Ryn?"

Aeden's voice began to quiver just a little bit like it did when she was younger and someone would hurt her feelings. I was about to answer but she kept talking.

"What about me? I'm not in any pictures. What if you go back in time and I don't? What do I tell Mom and Dad? What do I do?"

"Just because there aren't any photos of you doesn't mean you didn't go back with me. Besides, this is probably just a bunch of nonsense anyway."

"Then why even bother?"

"Because I'd rather try something and fail than spend the rest of my life wondering what would've happened. If you don't take chances, you might as well just sit around and rot."

"What if we don't come back?"

"We do. We're here now so that must mean we did."

Well, it sounded good anyway when I said it to reassure Aeden. But I knew even then it wasn't the truth.

Chapter Seven:

Aeden

Ryn was already taking the stuff out of the cardboard box when I walked into the big bedroom the next morning. Our parents made sure we had plenty of soft drinks and water in the fridge plus some fruit and crackers that we brought from the motel, just in case their meeting with the bank trustees went longer than expected.

I watched carefully as he scrutinized the different sized prisms before standing them up on the dresser.

"So what are we supposed to do with them?"

"Give me a sec, Aeden; I just want to read her notes again."

"You told me yesterday that her notes were about *Snell's Law*."

"They are. But she changed the formula and drew a diagram with small boxes and angles. See for yourself."

The formula made no sense to me. But honestly, neither did any of the formulas I had to learn for school. I just memorized them and plunked in the numbers that the teachers gave us to figure them out. But this was different. It had a drawing.

"I think the little boxes represent the prisms."

"Yeah, I think so, too," Ryn said as he arranged the prisms to match the diagram from Auntie Zanne's notes. Then, out of nowhere he let out a yell as if he'd been stung by a scorpion or something.

"WHAT? What's the matter?"

"I just got it, Aeden. I just figured it out. The prisms don't stand by themselves. We have to stand in the middle of them with enough sunlight to bounce off of them. Come on! Grab some of them and let's head outside."

Before I could say another word, my brother had a handful of prisms and was heading out the back door to the open yard and motioning for me to hurry up.

"There's a clear space over there by the small cactus plants. Every other spot in this yard is filled with junk. And I don't want to be taking any of it with us if we really do go through time."

"You mean you don't want any broken pottery or faded garden frogs?"

"I just don't want anything to get in the way. Now come on!"

He put the notes and the newspaper clipping in his pocket and arranged the prisms as if it were a chess game and everything had to be set up just right.

"Okay, Aeden. Let's see if old Auntie Zanne was seriously off her rocker or if she was really brilliant."

He grabbed my arm and had me stand directly in front of him as both of us stood in the middle of an octagon shape whose perimeter was defined by the prisms.

At first nothing happened.

"Give it a second," I heard Ryn say. "Light has to travel."

That was the last thing I heard before I collapsed, narrowly missing the prickly pear cactus that was taking over the yard.

It seemed as if hours had passed before I opened my eyes and tried to stand up. Everything felt wobbly as if the ground beneath me was moving. The vibrations were strong and steady, and I could smell coal, smoke and straw. I was moving. Well, I was at least on something that was moving. It just took me a minute or two in order to comprehend what it was. Worse yet, I didn't see Ryn.

It was unmistakable. The chugging and forward motion meant only one thing. I was on a train. But where and when, I had no idea. The compartment was only dimly lit by some shafts of light that came in from the seams in the walls. I was moving all right. But not through time. And I wasn't alone.

A girl's voice came out of nowhere and I felt every single hair on my body stand up as if death itself was about to greet me.

"So, you ditched the orphan train, too, huh? Didn't see you in that pile of straw. When did you catch this one? I've been riding it since Nebraska."

"Orphan train? Nebraska?"

"Yeah, didn't the good doers from the Children's Aid Society tell you they were putting you on the orphan train? Did you come from New York or Boston?"

My mind tried to grasp what was happening but everything seemed like a jumble of thoughts. Orphan trains? Not those! Where the heck is Ryn? But I'm not on that kind of train anymore. The girl said so. The prisms worked. Orphan trains were years ago. At least a hundred years ago. But what train am I on? And where's Ryn?

My mind was working at breakneck speed, trying to piece together what had happened; but my voice hadn't caught up with it.

"I...I, um, er..."

"Never mind, you don't have to say anything. I'm taking this train as far as Arizona and then getting off. I figure no one will be looking for me there. You can come along if you want, unless of course you plan on going all the way to California."

"No, I mean, no, I hadn't planned on California."

"Good. Then we'll jump off when we get to the first station in Arizona. Better get some sleep. We should be arriving pretty soon."

I leaned back into a scratchy pile of hay and listened to the monotonous thud of the train wheels, wondering what on earth I should do.

Chapter Eight:
Ryn

*T*he sound was soft at first, like some sort of clicking. But then it got louder and louder. Clackety-clackety-clackety…It droned in my ears until a whistle sliced through it and someone announced, "Next stop, Morenci, Arizona."

I was wedged between two boys who were both trying to lean out of the train's window. The railcar reeked of sweat and musty air, and all I could see were boys. Boys of all ages who were crawling, pushing and shoving to look out of the windows. No one seemed to notice how I got there and no one cared. Aeden was nowhere in sight. The only thing I remembered before finding myself here was standing behind her in the yard, surrounded by prisms and light.

This was awful. I never expected to be separated from her. I figured that if light could move us through time we'd be together. Poor Aeden. She must be panic stricken by now. And it was all my fault. Worse yet, I didn't know if she was in the same year, month and place as I was, or if time moved her somewhere else. The only thing I could do was look for her.

My knees bumped the kids who had moved toward the windows as I stood in the aisle to look for my sister. No use. There were no girls on this railcar. Just boys whose faces and clothing reminded me of the pictures I'd seen of the Great Depression. Then it hit me. My clothes! Someone will know immediately that I don't belong here. And then what? I was wearing jeans and an old white t-shirt and my sneakers were black and dirty. Tough luck. I was stuck and there was nothing I could do about it.

Another whistle blew and the conductor's voice followed it. "Coming Up. Morenci, Arizona!"

Someone jabbed my elbow and I turned to see who it was. A kid with the worst haircut I'd ever seen was staring right at me. Whoever got ahold of his head obviously was not too familiar with using a scissors. Before I could say anything, he spoke.

"You think you'll get a decent family?"

"A what? What do you mean?"

"You know, a good family. One that will feed you and give you clothes and not work the daylights out of you."

I was about to tell him that with the exception of having to hoe out my lunatic Auntie Zanne's house, I had a great family and plenty of food and clothes. But I didn't say a word so he just kept talking.

"I got picked up for lifting some fruit from a stand and next thing I know I'm in the city orphanage. And then on this train to find a family that'll take me. Got all cleaned up for the ride, too. Say, how come they didn't give you a shirt? You just got underwear on?"

I looked down and thought, "They think this is underwear? It's a t-shirt for cryin' out loud." Then I spoke.

"I don't know. I got separated from my sister and really need to find her."

"The girls will be in another railcar. You'll probably see 'em when we get off. But don't bet on being placed with her. That never happens."

The screech of the brakes pierced my ears as I was thrust forward in my seat. Next thing I knew, the train had come to a complete stop and we were told to get down and wait on the platform.

There must have been at least 30 or 40 of us, but before I could break away to see if I could find Aeden, the conductor and two official looking men directed us to line up by height and not utter a word . Line up by height? Last time I remembered doing something as idiotic as that was when I was in second grade and we had to pick partners for pee-wee wrestling in gym.

We stood in a long line, the sweat from the Arizona heat dripping in our eyes. One by one, people walked up to us and looked carefully. I could hear them talking.

"That one's too skinny. Won't be much help."

"There's a tall one over there but he seems kind of sickly."

"Check the arms and faces and make sure they don't have a rash."

Was this how the slaves felt when they were sold at city auctions? And then I thought about Aeden. She'd be crying by now. Quickly, I darted out of the line and ran down the platform to where the girls were standing in their straight column. Aeden had been wearing a silly little pinafore dress with tiny yellow flowers. I know, because I teased her about it. My eyes scanned for that dress but it wasn't there. No yellow-flowered dress. No Aeden. I was about to say something to one of the girls in the line when someone grabbed my arm and yanked me so hard that I almost fell.

"What the heck do you think you're doing, kid? Get back in that line. Trash like you are lucky someone will pick them up. Understand? Now get back in line."

There was no place to run. The train was still on the tracks and the station had guards posted around it. I walked slowly back without saying a word. Then I heard a woman's voice from behind me.

"He's about the same size as Albert was. 'Bout the same age, too."

A man answered her.

"Won't cost us much. He'll be able to fit in Albert's old clothes."

"You sure you want to do this?"

"Farm ain't gonna run itself. We need the help, Dora. I say we take him."

They walked away for a minute, but returned with one of the officials who appeared to be checking my name off of a list. He shook his head and shrugged.

"What's your name, son?"

My voice was barely audible. "Ryn."

"Ren?" "Don't see anyone named Ren, but...oh yeah, let's see, there's a Rendell listed here. Must be him. All set."

Before I could say anything else, the man and woman motioned for me to follow them. We walked through the station house and down the steps to a small gravel filled parking lot before the man spoke.

"Truck's over there. Don't take all day. We've got a long ride back to the farm."

I'd seen pictures of 1920's trucks before, but never the real thing. I walked towards it slowly, trying to figure out how to get in the back.

The man was getting impatient.

"What's the matter with you, Rendell, ain't they got trucks back in New York City? Or is this one not modern enough for the likes of you? Now come on. Get in."

I watched the road moving away from me as I leaned back against the cab of the truck. All I could think about was Aeden. Where had she gone? Was she all right? And how was I going to find her?

The man drove slowly, navigating the switch back curves and mountain drop-offs as if he had done this forever. My head started to feel light and I closed my eyes, allowing the rocking motion to lull me to sleep. It would be the only good sleep I was to have for a long time.

Chapter Nine:
Aeden

I must have dozed off because next thing I knew someone was shaking me. I couldn't hear what they were saying because the sound of the train coming to a stop overpowered their voice. As I turned my head I could see it was the girl. Maybe my age. Maybe a bit older. She had long, curly dark hair that hung just below her shoulders and was wearing some sort of pinafore dress that you'd see in old magazines. Really old magazines.

"Hurry up. Give me a hand opening the latch on the door. We've got to jump and make a run for it before anyone sees us!"

"Jump? Run?"

"Yeah. How'd you expect we'd get off this train? We're not exactly ticket holding passengers. Now come on! Quick, before anyone sees us!"

My eyes were immediately blinded by the bright sunshine as the girl released the metal latch and started to open the door. It must have weighed a ton because both of us had to lean all of our weight on it to get it to inch forward. In the narrow space that we had managed to open, the girl tossed a rolled up object to the ground and gave me a shove.

"JUMP! NOW!"

I felt my knees move forward before I suddenly realized that I was no longer in the railcar. Hurling myself forward, I landed on hard dirt ground. The girl was directly behind me.

"Okay. Good! Now let's make a run for it!"

She grabbed the rolled-up object which I could now see was some sort of large rag-bag that held all of her belongings. Then, she motioned for me to follow as we ran behind the station house and over a small rocky hill.

"Train'll be gone in a few minutes, once they unload the cattle and passengers so we really need to hurry."

I was still voiceless. It was as if I was participating in a dream with no will of my own. The girl, however, seemed to know exactly what she was doing.

"We're heading to the mines. Copper mines. Place is full of them. And you know what the out-product is? It's gold! GOLD! I figure we can get ourselves jobs as cooks and cleaners for the miners and in our own time, do some exploring. Most everyone, 'cept for a few in this country, are as poor as church mice, but I don't intend to be one of them."

My feet followed hers like a newly hatched bird that was imprinting on its mother. I was so scared, so confused and so lost that I needed someone to take control for a while, and Ryn wasn't here. I just prayed he would find me. The girl must have seen that empty look in my eyes because she slowed down for a minute and spoke to me as if we were somehow connected.

"Don't be scared. We'll be fine. Some of the miners come down this way to get supplies before they return to the mine. We'll hitch a ride with one of them. Tell them we're cooks and cleaners. They won't ask questions. They don't have time to make their own meals and wash their own clothes. They're too busy mining copper for the big companies and searching for gold on their own time."

My voice was high pitched and raspy but at least it came back.

"My brother. I'm missing my brother. I don't know where he is."

"He didn't jump the orphan train like you did? I don't know why I asked that. You wouldn't know. The boys and girls travel on separate cars. Look, if he jumped the train, we'd spot him. If not, some family probably adopted him and he's on his way to their place. It's a large territory, but not that populated. We'll keep our eyes open. Okay?"

I nodded, still too overwhelmed to speak.

"So, what's your name, anyway?"

"Aeden."

"Funny name. Mine's Sue. No sense asking for last names. We'll never know our real names anyway. Come on. Looks like some miners are up ahead on the road. I'll try to convince them to take us to their camp."

"Sue! Wait!"

"What is it?"

"I don't know how to cook."

"Yeah, but they know how to eat and I don't think it much matters."

By late afternoon we had arrived at the Phelps Dodge Morenci Copper Mine where Sue and I joined some older women as cleaners and cooks. The only thing I remember was scrubbing pots until my hands felt raw. I collapsed onto my cot that night, but not before catching a glimpse of Sue opening her rag bag and sorting out some objects— pieces of broken glass, a horseshoe magnet, string, some long nails, a small notebook, an old colored pencil and a narrow gold pin with a light blue stone set into the design on top. It didn't take me long to realize that the girl I had followed was no ordinary orphan.

Chapter Ten:
Ryn

*T*he truck sputtered to a stop and I opened my eyes. We were in the hills somewhere, isolated from anything you'd call civilization. A small one story house with crumbling adobe, a deteriorating garage and a barn were the only buildings in sight. I could see a fenced-in area next to the barn with goats and a horse. A few chickens roamed freely.

"So, this is what hell looks like," I thought to myself as I jumped down from the truck bed and onto the dirt driveway. I wasn't about to wait for anyone to give me orders. My mind seemed to be working overtime processing what had happened in the last few hours.

Things were beginning to get clearer in my head. I figured that Aeden had to be somewhere close by because she was right in front of me when the light from the prisms bounced us back in time. She fell forward, but still within the same spectrum of light. I reasoned that she had to be in the same time as me just separated by distance. But where? There was no time to waste. As soon as I had the opportunity, I was gonna get the hell out of here and start looking.

I was pissed at Auntie Zanne and even more teed-off at myself for actually taking such a stupid chance. Well, my parents didn't have to worry about me smoking or doing drugs, and I was too young to drink and drive, but who woulda thought I'd wind up time tripping with no end in sight? My parents never lectured us about that one. A loud voice came from nowhere and I looked up.

"Rendell, Miss Dora will show you where you're going to sleep and give you a glass of water. Then you get back out here to start stacking wood. We don't have all day. Couldn't get all the chores done since we had to drive to Morenci to get you. Now hurry on."

A softer voice followed.

"Couldn't the boy rest a little? He must be tired from the train ride and the drive here."

"I'm tired, too, Dora. We're all tired. But the work ain't gonna wait and he'll have to get used to it."

I've taken out garbage, mowed lawns, shoveled snow and helped my dad with re-cycling and all sorts of projects, but I never learned how to stack firewood. It wasn't something we did. Our house in Portland was heated by electricity. But I learned fast. I had to. Yeah, believe it or not, there's actually a right way to stack firewood and after getting yelled at and slapped behind the head a few times by the man who "adopted" me, I figured it out.

It was just about dusk when I finished and walked back into the house. Miss Dora motioned for me to sit at the small kitchen table with her and her husband. She doled out some sort of corn soup with bacon and a slice of bread. Water was the only thing we had to drink but who cared? I was tired, thirsty, and would have eaten anything. The sound of my own teeth biting on the hard bread was the only thing I heard until the man started speaking. He looked at me with a mix of need and hatred. A look I never forgot.

"Need to get a few things straight, Rendell. Don't think you're gonna be going to school because there's no time for that. You've had all the schooling you're gonna need and besides, it's too far from the farm. You'll be working here with me. Lots to do. Understand?"

I nodded. I mean, what the heck was I supposed to do? I was driven by two thoughts and held on to them like a pit bull on a steak. GET THE HELL OUT OF HERE AND FIND AEDEN.

After dinner, Miss Dora showed me my room and pointed out a dresser with shirts and pants that I could wear.

"Get some sleep, Rendell," she said. "Tomorrow's gonna come awfully soon."

It wasn't much of a room. Just a small narrow bed and the dresser. I could see places on the wall where someone had taped pictures but they were long gone. Only the sticky remains of where the tape held them gave any indication of life in this crummy bedroom. Old green curtains hung on the only window. I immediately went over and lifted it. It worked! And as much as I knew it was dangerous and stupid to be out in the hills at night, I had no choice if I was to escape from my new "family." If this is what life was like for the poor kids on the orphan train, no wonder it was all but buried in the history books.

I waited until I was sure everyone was asleep. Until I couldn't hear any sounds from the house. I was lucky. A full moon lit up the sky and I could see the dirt road ahead. The window creaked a bit, but not enough to wake anyone. I moved fast, jumping from the sill to the ground and sprinting down the road. Unlike the desert, it was cool at night in the hills. Something was going my way after all, or so I thought. Funny, but when you think you feel the safest, is the time you should be the most worried. I found out too late.

Chapter Eleven:

Aeden

Salty tears that had found their way into my mouth woke me up from a winding, endless dream. A chase and shadows. Ryn, running for his life. Ryn, only inches away from something. Something dangerous. Something awful. I couldn't see it. I just knew it. But then, in an instant, it was gone, like all dreams. I sat up in my cot and wiped the tears from my face.

"Sue," I whispered. "Sue. I have to find my brother. I can't wait."

"Shush. Don't want anyone to hear us. You can't go running off looking for him. It's not safe. But we'll find him. Honestly, if he got on that stinking train, we'll find him. Now go back to sleep. They're going to be waking us up before you know it."

A quick rustling sound and Sue had turned away from me. Back to sleep in her cot. I felt my lower lip tremble and forced myself not to cry. I never did get back to sleep. I just kept thinking about the prisms, how we got separated and that terrifying dream. I was actually thankful to be washing dishes and shucking corn the next day. There were ten of us women and girls who worked in the mine kitchen, so it made it hard to talk privately with Sue. It wasn't until after the lunch shift when the others went back to their cots to rest, that Sue pulled me aside to show me her rag-bag and tell me her plan.

"You don't think I got off the train and came to these mines by accident, now, do you? I told you about the gold. Now I'm going to explain how we're about to mine some for ourselves."

"But it's not our gold. It belongs to Phelps Dodge."

"They've got enough. Besides, I can always return it someday when I've made something of myself."

"What do you mean?"

"You think I want to live the rest of my life working with my bare hands when it's my mind that should be used? I plan to get enough gold so that I can sell it, get back to New York and pay for an education. Colleges are taking girls now. Haven't you heard?"

"Boy, if she only knew," I thought to myself as Sue continued talking.

"I can read and write, do math and I know a lot of stuff about science."

"You do? How?"

"The libraries are free. I used to spend hours in the science section when I wasn't out on the street panhandling for money."

"Didn't you ever have a family?"

"I was placed in a city orphanage when I was really young, so I don't know. But I ran away one day and started living on the streets. That was before child welfare and humanitarian services found me and returned me. Then, the orphan train and you know the rest. Here we are. What about you?"

"I don't want to talk about it. I just want to find my brother."

"Look, I understand. I do. But we've got to get enough gold so that we can leave here and really ask around for your brother. Okay?"

"Yeah, Okay. So how do we get this gold? What are we looking for? And won't we get caught?"

"We won't get caught if we get into the untouched areas of the mines. And I'll show you what to look for and what to do. All you need is a nail and a rag to carry out the gold.”

“But what about lights? How will we see?”

“We just take one of the lanterns from another area. Stop worrying. I really thought about this carefully. It’ll work. It has to.”

Chapter Twelve:
Ryn

****

The man woke before sunup and pounded twice on the door to Ryn's room.

"Up Rendell. Work ain't gonna wait!" Silence. Again a fist to the door and a quick kick to open it.

"Dora! Boy's done and left. Never slept here."

But before she could answer, the man walked straight back to his bedroom and grabbed the 12 gauge shotgun that was propped against a small closet. As he approached the hallway, his wife's eyes darted from the gun to his face.

"You're not going to do anything you'll regret."

"Gonna do what I have to. Didn't waste a day and hard earned money to have that snit of a boy bolt on us."

"He's just a kid."

"A kid who should've known better. And someone's gonna teach him."

Dora wrung her hands together as she watched her husband leave the house and get into the truck. The sound of crunching stone under the tires gradually disappeared, and with it, any hopes she might have had for Ryn returning to their household.

****

I slipped past the house and down the dirt road. Slowly, at first, so as not to make any noise. Then, I picked up speed as my sneaks bounced over the small rocks. I was lucky. The moon was huge, shaped like an ice cream scoop, and there were a zillion stars. Were they always this bright? I knew I had to get back to the train station and start looking for Aeden.

And as much as I didn't want to start thinking about it, all I could picture was her cleaning and washing and scrubbing for some lousy family that wanted free slave labor. And Aeden wouldn't complain. She'd just do it. 'Cause that's the way she is. She'd wait it out, hoping for me to find her and to get released back in time. Poor Aeden. I could see her crying and biting her nails when no one was looking.

Okay, so it was really a stupid thing for us to do to begin with. But I have my theories about time travel, too. And nature. And the universe. I think things belong in a certain time and place, and that nature or whatever you want to call it, will do whatever it has to, in order to make sure that everything is where it belongs. Including Aeden and me. *Balance.* The word was on the tip of my tongue. We're out of balance in this time and something will bring us back. But I've got to find her first.

My legs were getting sore and I still hadn't gotten to the main road. Then, I heard it. A quiet squeak at first, like the sound you'd expect a mouse to make, but this was some big mouse. And then more squeaks until it became recognizable from somewhere back in my mind. I was eight or nine and on a camping trip in Eugene with my dad, my friend Larry's dad, and the scouts from Troop 12. I hadn't thought about that night in years. But as the high pitched sounds got closer and closer, I remembered what kind of sounds they were.

"Shh, don't move. Just listen. It's coyotes and they've just made a kill. Hear that yipping, squeaking sound? That's the sound they make when they've just killed something."

"It's creepy, Dad. I wanna go back to the tent."

"You'll be all right, Ryn. They're not after you. It's a small kill. Probably a rabbit or badger, or some other unfortunate creature that couldn't get away."

"But rabbits are fast, Dad."

"Yeah, but not when they're surrounded by coyotes."

"What do I do if a coyote comes after me?"

"Yell, wave your arms, make him think he has a reason to be scared, clap your hands and do whatever it takes to get it to move on. Even throw rocks at him. But stop worrying, Ryn. A coyote isn't going to attack you."

Now, I was all alone. My dad was in another time and place and I had no idea if I was going to be the next target for a kill. I ran faster. The yipping, squeaking sounds seemed to fade as I reached the main road. Which way? Which way takes me back to the station? It was all so dark and confusing. Then I remembered. We turned right when we went up the drive. So that meant go left. Still a dirt road, but this one was wide and the dirt was packed down solid. I pushed myself and kept running.

Then, somewhere from behind me I heard it. A soft howl at first, but a howl. No time to turn and look. Run, Ryn, run! It was all hill and bush, pine-like trees and mounds. I thought I saw some sort of structure a few yards away and headed straight towards it. A house! It was someone's house. All dark and quiet for the night, but someone's house. If this were ordinary circumstances I would've pounded their door down to get inside, that's how freaking scared I was. Only I knew that they'd send for a sheriff and that I'd never escape from this hell.

I kept running, only allowing myself to take a quick glance at the house. And that's when I saw it. It was propped against the front porch waiting for someone to grab its handlebars, fling a leg over the seat and get moving. I was that someone. Yeah, yeah, stealing is bad. I know. But I didn't have many choices. I'd ditch the bike once I got to the town.

Everything about it was thick and clumsy from its tires to the heavy handlebars and metal. And it was long, too. Much longer than my Marin Bayview Trail bike. I felt awkward, out of whack, but still, it was a bike and I knew how to ride. Sorry kid, if this was your transport to school or whatever, you'll just have to walk. Me? I'm running; make that riding, for my life.

The road went on forever and so did the night. What took a few hours in the car took me until daylight. An empty train station and now what? I leaned the bike next to the side of the building, but not before touching its handlebars and taking a closer look. It was red. Faded red with chipped metal. Maybe it had been loved once, but now it was used up, like I would've been if I stayed.

"I'm no thief," I whispered to the bike. "There's another word for me; and I think it's *fugitive*."

A worn wooden sign across from the train station pointed to the Morenci Mines. It would be a start. I could hitch a ride with someone and ask around. Mining was a big operation in Arizona back then. Lots of people working. Lots of families to support. Someone must have seen Aeden. Someone must know where she is. Then, it hit me and I felt the salty saliva creep into my mouth. That guy would be looking for me. I couldn't wait to hitch a ride. I'd have to get to the mines before the station opened.

"Sorry bike," I muttered. "Your kid will just have to wait it out."

Chapter Thirteen:

Aeden

"**Y**ou can't just use the rock to chip away at the vein. You'll have to use your fingernails, too."

It was just past dusk. The miners had eaten and we were done with dish washing and pan scrubbing. Sue and I slipped away from the makeshift mining camp and headed down the road to the mine itself. No one else was around. The miners were probably exhausted. Beside, who in their right mind would be going into a deep, dark hole at night? Who indeed? I was petrified. All I could think of was coal miners who got trapped underground and suffocated to death. Sue must have sensed that as she watched me take tentative steps.

"Aeden, we can walk right into this mine. It's not like we need to get on some elevator or take one of those coal mining trains down in the depths. It's just a series of channels and passages cut into the mountain. Honest. It's not scary at all."

"What if we get lost?"

"We can't get lost if we know our left from our right. We just keep track. Once we get inside, we look for one of the wall lanterns. Some of them will still be lit. We just take it and work our way down one of the passages. Once we see a copper vein, we'll know where to look for the gold."

"You'll know. I won't."

"I'll show you. Stop worrying."

Sue was right. There was no elevator or cavernous drop-off. Just ambling passages in the dark. It was cool and dry inside. I took a deep breath but all I could smell was earth and rock. A heady, deep smell that seemed to be as old as time... We "flecked" the gold chips easily and watched them drop to the ground. Sue snatched them up and dropped them into her rag-bag like a kindergartener grabbing Halloween treats.

It was quiet in the mine. Creepy, eerie quiet. Not the kind of quiet like when you're out camping. The woods have a life to them. But the mine...it felt dead. And I strained to hear any kind of sound. Nothing.

"Come on, Aeden, we've got to find a different vein. We don't have hammers and picks to get any further with this one. Got to get going."

The night seemed to last forever, even though it was just a few hours. We went from vein to vein in the first passage. Sue, gathering her flecks and chips. Me, just hoping there would be enough gold dust to help get me closer to Ryn.

"I'm getting tired, Sue. Can we just take a break? And I'm thirsty."

"There's a pump and a well out in front of the mine. We'll head back, get a drink and then continue."

Holding the lantern in front of me, my pace quickened as we got closer to the exit.

"It's over there, about 15 feet to the left. Do you see it?"

It was just like the pump back at the camp. A few metal cups were lying on the ground underneath the lever. I tried not to think about germs and bacteria as I let the water fill the cup. It smelled metallic but I gulped it down quickly. And then I had the strangest sensation as if Ryn were right next to me. Close enough to touch, close enough to absorb...Musky, sweaty, like sneakers and old deodorant. Ryn... I sipped more water, trying to hold on to the moment before Sue snatched it from me when she reached for the cup.

"Okay, we'd better get a move on. Let's take the small passage off to the right this time. It's narrower but not by much."

I wasn't as scared of the mine this time. It had let me in and let me out. Sue was a few feet ahead of me, talking about how much gold was really available if we had the right tools.

I didn't say a word. I just nodded in the dark and kept moving. Sue was always a few feet ahead and I struggled to keep up. First, a few feet, then a few yards. I started to take larger strides. That's when I heard a thud and saw Sue trip over something.

"Damn it!" she yelled. "What the …? Aeden, hurry, shine the lantern here!"

"Did you fall over a big rock or what?"

"I'm not sure. It didn't feel like a rock."

Just as I outstretched my arm to move the lantern closer, I heard her gasp.

"Oh my God, Oh my God. It's a body, Aeden. A dead body!"

I didn't want to look down but the more I forced myself not to, the urge to look got stronger. I closed my eyes but that didn't help. The urge was still there. I thought that if I were to open my eyes slowly, it wouldn't be too bad. I was wrong. Like a spotlight for a stage performer, the lantern illuminated the body. It was a man. I covered my mouth with my hand, turned and raced out of the passageway with Sue directly behind me.

Off to the side of the mine, I threw up. I've never seen a dead body before. And the few funerals that I had attended were closed casket. I just stood there in the dark, feeling waves of nausea. My mouth was mothy and the words came out slowly.

"Should we go and tell someone?"

"Are you crazy? We're not supposed to be here, let alone stealing chips of gold. Next thing you know we'll be back in some orphanage or worse. We can't say anything. But I'm going back in to take another look."

"Take another look? What the heck for?"

"It may be someone we recognize."

"So?"

"So there had to be a reason why he was murdered."

"What makes you think he was murdered? Maybe he just had a heart attack and dropped dead."

"You didn't look very carefully, Aeden, did you? 'Cause if you did, you would've seen the blood coming out of his chest. Someone either shot him or stabbed him. But I think they shot

him, because he'd have lots more blood all over
him if someone used a knife."

"I'm not going back in."

"Fine. Stand out here and wait. Just give me
the lantern."

"What if whoever killed him is still in the
mine?"

"They're not. We would have heard
something. The body's probably been here all
day."

"Just hurry up, will you?"

I watched the light from the lantern cut a
trail as Sue walked back to the mine. Then I sat
down by the pump and waited, too numb to do
anything else. Something shiny seemed to
catch my eye as the lantern light moved further
down the path. Maybe Sue had dropped a small
chip of gold.

As I bent down to see what it was, I felt every
hair on my back stand up. Ryn! Ryn must have
been here. It was the small plastic nub from the
tip of a shoelace and they didn't have plastic
tips back then…

Chapter Fourteen:

Ryn

The road to the mine was rocky, uphill and long. Still, I had no choice. Forcing myself to push harder and harder on the pedals, I felt every stinkin' muscle in my legs. So this is life in the late 20's or 30's. Well, it rots. I would've gone ballistic for a lousy three-speed bike. But hey, beggars can't be choosers or whatever the heck that expression is. And I was thirsty. Really thirsty, so when I saw the water pump in front of the mine, I jumped down from my bike and started to make a dash for it.

Damn! My shoe lace got caught in one of the spokes and ripped the tip off. No big deal. I grabbed one of the metal cups, pumped the lever and started to fill it. Then I drank and drank until the water dripped down my chin and across my shirt. I don't ever remember being that thirsty.

The entrance to the mine was wide open. Guess they didn't need security back then. "What the heck," I thought to myself, "might as well take a peek inside until the miners get here. Then I can ask around if anyone had seen Aeden."

I stepped inside. Funny, some of the lanterns were lit and that made no sense to me, unless of course, miners were here already. I rushed in. At first I didn't hear anything, but then, all of a sudden, I heard voices and for some reason, I could make out every word. Maybe it had something to do with sound waves in tunnels, who the heck knows, but anyway, what I heard was more like the dialogue from one of those corny black and white Westerns that my grandfather used to watch. Short sentences. Short and to the point.

"They'll figure out the gold is missing and they'll be after you."

"By the time they come lookin' I'll be long gone."

"You won't get away with it."

"I already have."

And then, a shot! I could feel my body jolt seconds before the ringing in my ears started. A shot! HOLY SH...! Someone shot someone and here I am a few feet away! Hell, if they could do that, then they'll think nothing of shooting me!

I turned and started to run out of the mine as if a zillion Africanized bees were about to swarm me. And that's when I realized that the killer would see me. So I darted into one of the smaller tunnels, pressed myself against the wall and waited. Why was my breathing so damn loud? It sounded like an old tugboat making its way into the harbor. An old tugboat that was about to get its ass blown up.

The more I tried, the harder it was to get my breathing slowed down. And just when I thought I had things under control, I heard footsteps. I swear I thought my heart was about to crash out of my chest. The footsteps were coming my way and I had no place to go, except deeper into the mine. Great. Then whoever it was would kill me too and no one would ever know. I put my hand over my mouth and stayed still. I could hear the footsteps but they changed direction. They weren't headed my way. I could wait this out. But then, for some reason, some inexplicable reason that I'll never understand 'cause it crosses that fine line between bravery and insanity, I decided to follow the sound and see who the murderer was. I had to admit that it was right up there with all the other stupid things I've done. In fact, it may have taken first place.

The sound was getting fainter but still audible. The killer was heading out of the mine. No time to waste. I walked as quickly as I could without making too much noise. And I walked against the side of the tunnel figuring that if someone turned around, they wouldn't be as likely to see me. I was wrong. Wrong enough to be face to face with a murderer. My hands felt clammy and I swear my heart was going to explode. I had to think fast.

"Hey, mister!" I yelled. "I'm looking for my sister. She's lost. Have you seen a young girl about 12 years old?"

The man eyed me and took a step forward. He was younger than my dad with broad shoulders and brownish hair and looked as if he hadn't shaved in a few days. Nothing out of the ordinary. I mean, it's not as if killers look like killers. He just looked normal. A guy with a buttoned down beige shirt and jeans. He could've been someone's coach, or a teacher. But he wasn't. I took a deep breath and asked again.

"So, have you seen her? I've been looking all over."

By now we were both outside of the mine. The man took a quick look behind him and then faced me before he spoke.

"That your bike over there?"

I froze. What if that guy recognized the bike? What if it belonged to his kid? He'd know I was a liar. And then, what? So I answered as directly as possible.

"That's the bike I rode over here to find my sister. I've been riding all over the place."

"What were you doing in the mine?"

"Like I said, I'm looking for my sister. Her name is Aeden and she's lost. I thought she might have wandered into the mine but I called for her and there was no answer. Then I heard your footsteps."

"What else did you hear?"

"Nothing."

"I haven't seen your sister, kid. Sorry. Stay out of the mine. Understand? Too dangerous if you know what I mean. And if I were you, I'd get on the bike and start looking elsewhere."

I nodded. The guy was giving me a break and I knew it. At least I hoped he was giving me a break. Without wasting a second, I made a run for the bike. And that's when I saw the truck. The truck with the man who had "adopted" me at the train station. A quick slam of the door and he was headed my way.

I had to think fast. This was not going to be one of those "character counts" moments when you weigh each decision and make your choice. Is this the right decision for me and my family? Will anyone be hurt by my decision? Does this decision fit with my future goals? What the hell! I had a murderer on one side of me and a slave driver on the other. I made my choice and walked back towards the mine.

"I lied mister. I heard everything. The shot, the other guy. Everything. And you can't kill me. At least not right here and not right now. Look! People are showing up. The miners are coming. So take me with you!"

The guy could see the old man getting out of the truck. But when the old guy reached back inside for a shotgun, that's when the killer grabbed me by the scruff of my shirt and yanked me forward.

"Hurry up! Got a horse tied up just beyond the knoll. Run for it!"

I moved faster than I ever thought was possible. I could see a reddish brown horse with a white blaze behind some scrub brush. And the killer was just a few steps ahead of me. He was already untying the horse from a small tree and jumping on. He held out his hand to give me a lift.

"Come on. Haven't you gotten on a horse before?"

I've been on skateboards, bikes, razor scooters, and even a motorcycle. But a horse? Where was I going to ride a horse in Portland? I never even got to ride a pony as a kid. And the thing was big. Tall. I saw the open stirrup, shoved my left foot into it and let the guy lift me up. In seconds I was holding on to his waist as the horse made a grunting sound, kicked up some dirt and started to move. Uphill. Uphill at first. I glanced back. There was no way a car could follow us. We were riding over terrain, not a road. The guy with the shotgun wasn't going to get free labor from me today. Instead, I was holding onto a murderer and praying I wasn't going to be his next target.

Chapter Fifteen:

Aeden

I squeezed the plastic shoelace tip in my fist until my hand started to hurt. Then I carefully put it in the front pocket of my sundress and sat on the ground. My eyes started to tear and I wished Sue would hurry up because I knew that once I started to cry, I probably wouldn't stop. What could be taking her so long? The thought of looking at a dead body made me nauseous. Why she had to go see who it was made no sense at all. But then again, everything she did seemed strange. I let out a long breath and waited. Finally she came running out of the mine clutching her rag-bag under the arm and yelling.

"It was no one I recognized. But we did get lucky. Look!"

Unfolding the cloth bag, Sue held up a small black sock that appeared to be weighted down.

She untied the knot that held it together and thrust the contents under my nose.

"Gold! You found a bag of gold?"

"Yep! Not just flecks. Not just chips. Real solid chunks of gold! The guy must've stashed it, figuring he'd come back for it. The sock was off to the side on a small dirt ledge. The only reason I found it was because I put my hand on the ledge to lean in and get a better look at the body. He probably put it there before he got shot."

"But that's stealing! You can't just take the gold!"

"Stealing? From who? A dead guy? He's not going to need it."

"But maybe he has a family; maybe they need the money, maybe…"

"Oh for heaven's sakes, Aeden, he probably stole that money himself and that's what got him killed."

"Still, I think we should…"

"Should what? Tell someone back at the camp? Then we'll be in trouble for going into the mine and the last thing we need is for someone to call the county sheriff. Want real trouble? We'll wind up in another orphanage. Listen, I know you want to find your brother. Well, now we're in a better position to do so. But first, we have to get to a county assayers office, find out what this is worth and get a real bank account. And we can't do that in this county."

"What do you mean?"

"They'll know that it came from a local mine. And they'll know it doesn't belong to us. We've got to go where they won't ask too many questions. And that leaves us two choices: Tucson or Mexico. Tucson's a pretty big city with lots of mining action. They won't know where the gold originated. And Mexico, well, trust me, they won't be asking us any questions."

"Of course they won't," I stammered. "We don't speak Spanish."

"So that leaves Tucson."

"Tucson," I muttered softly.

"It's a long way from here but I figure we can finish out the week working and use the money we get paid to get there."

"How?"

"We hitch a ride with one of the miners on the weekend. They're always heading to Safford or Thatcher. We'll tell them we have family there and miss them. No reason for them not to believe us. Then, we'll hitch south until we get to the main road to Tucson. It'll take a few days but so what?"

I just stood there looking at Sue. I kept reminding myself that this wasn't the 21st century and that hitchhiking wasn't dangerous, stupid, idiotic, or forbidden. The words my parents used whenever they spoke about it. I mean, after all, we did hitch a ride to the mining camp from the station and nothing bad happened. Still, I could hear my mother's voice.

"If you and Ryn ever do something like that, then you'll get what you deserve for not using your brains."

But this wasn't my time, or my place, and the girl I was following seemed to have all the answers. But how could she help me find Ryn? That was one question that needed an immediate response.

"But what if my brother is somewhere around here? Going miles away won't help me find him."

"Look, Aeden, we'll still be here for a few more days. We'll keep asking around. But Tucson's a big city. They have a newspaper and even a radio station. With the money we get, we can take out a personal ad. Lots of people read the paper. Someone's bound to have seen him."

"I just wish we could go to the sheriff or..."

"You know we can't. They'll ask too many questions. And we'd better keep our lips tight when we hitch. We'll just have to pretend that we're on our way to live with an aunt, or cousin. Meanwhile our biggest problem is making sure no one gets their hands on the gold. Either you or I will have to be watching this bag at all times."

I looked at the rag-bag and wondered what could be so all fired important about the bits and pieces of worthless stuff that she had collected. Sure, the gold was valuable, but broken glass? String? A chipped pencil? If I was going to hitch with Sue all the way to Tucson, then she should at least let me in on her secrets. I wet my lips and spoke.

"Why do you carry all those bits and pieces of things around? It's not like they're worth anything."

"They are to me."

"Why?"

"Because I own them and no one else does. Someday I'm going to have a place of my own where my things will never leave. I won't let go of them like someone did to me."

I thought I saw tears welling up in her large brown eyes, but she turned away from me, her voice slapping my face like a cold wind.

"Hurry up; we'd better get back to the mining camp."

Chapter Sixteen:

Ryn

*U*phill. Past the mining plateau and the reddish brown rocks. It seemed as if the horse would never tire. But then, as the terrain started to change and green brush appeared, we stopped and the guy turned to face me.

"Get down. Horse needs a break."

I leaned to the left, moved a leg behind me and managed to jump down. Clumsy, but at least I didn't fall. The guy was off the horse in a fast, singular motion.

"There's a small stream a few yards to the right. Horse needs to drink. You might want to do the same."

"Great," I thought to myself. "I'll drink murky water from some stream and then die of a parasitic infection or some unknown bacteria." I mean, yeah, it was early into the 20th century, but didn't they know about germs back then? Well, I was in no position to shed some light on the subject, and I was thirsty. I walked to the stream, bent down and cupped my hands. The water was cold, crisp and metallic. "Wonderful," I mumbled. "Maybe I'll die of lead poisoning."

A voice broke into my thoughts.

"We'll rest the horse for a few minutes and then get going."

I didn't say a word. Not when I got back on the horse and not when my rear end felt as if it was burned to the saddle. We kept riding. Following the stream. Another break for the horse. This time, I did unglue myself from the horse and topple to the ground. My butt was numb and raw. The guy reached out his hand to help me up but didn't say anything either. Not as if I expected him to. I mean, what was he going to say? That he just killed someone? I kind of figured that one out for myself.

It was late afternoon when I saw smoke at a distance. We had arrived to wherever we were supposed to. As it turned out, it was a small cabin with an adjacent lean-to that held a few more horses.

"Time to get down, kid. Wait for me by the cabin. I've got to water the horse and get him settled."

I did as I was told. Not like I had too many options. I knew someone had to be inside the building but I wasn't gonna be the one to walk in unannounced. For all I knew, another murderer was waiting, gun in hand. So, I stood still. Only my eyes moved as I took in my surroundings.

This was just the kind of place my dad would have loved for a camping weekend. With small pines trees, lots of rocky paths and a stream, he would have been in his glory. Some camping weekend! The truth of the matter was that I had just been taken to some killer's hideout where I imagined they'd tie me up. Yeah, I've seen enough movies. First some big Brutus of a guy will tell me I have nothing to worry about, and then his partner will figure out how to kill me and bury the body. And forget about trying to escape on a horse. I didn't know the first thing about putting a saddle on it, let alone grabbing the reins! Nope. I was stuck. My only hope was to tell such an elaborate lie that they would be forced to believe me and spare my life. But what? I got so caught up in my own thoughts that I didn't see the guy until he stepped onto the small porch and looked directly at me.

"Stay outside and don't move. I need to speak with my partners."

He grabbed the old door knob, pushed the wooden frame forward and disappeared inside. I took a few steps back on the porch until I stood directly in front of a cloudy glass window. Its curtains were so ratty that it was easy for me to sneak a quick look. Easy, but stupid. What if they saw me? Then what? I took my chances and wished I hadn't. The killer's partners made the Incredible Hulk look like a wimp. I was dead meat. It was just a matter of time.

And then I did something even dumber. I put my ear to the glass and listened. Wished I hadn't 'cause no one wants to hear what I did.

"... shot dead. Kid saw me. Just... try to get away."

I jumped back and stumbled toward the edge of the porch just as the door swung open. Yep, I was dead meat. It was just a matter of time, or in this case, minutes.

Chapter Seventeen:

Aeden

We guarded the gold for five days as we tried to ask around about Ryn, but no one in the mining camp had seen anyone who resembled him. So I agreed to go with her to Tucson. No one asked any questions. No one cared. We got paid for the work we did and got up early the next day to start hitching rides.

The lies slipped, tumbled and rolled out of her mouth like the quarry rocks we saw on the way to Safford. She could make anyone believe anything, especially me. So it was no wonder that the people we hitched rides with never questioned anything.

"On our way to stay with an aunt in Thatcher."

"Mother is ill. Father is working the mines. Going to stay with family in Wilcox."

"Lost our money. It was all our dad gave us."

And on it went. From Morenci to Wilcox, Benson to Tucson, and everyplace in-between, once people looked into those big brown eyes of Sue's it was like they were hypnotized. Beguiled. Deceived. Call it whatever you want, but she had a way of making the people around her do whatever she wanted them to do. I watched and learned.

The roads were mostly dirt and gravel and the trucks and cars we rode in seemed to break down at least once or twice. Flat tires. Oil leaks. Engine trouble. But whatever the problem, the driver seemed to be able to fix it.

It took us days to get there. Days of sleeping in barns, outside porches and lean-tos. Most people were nice and fed us what little they had. A piece of bread with butter. Dried beef jerky. Beans. Corn. I moved about like a shadow of myself, unattached, disconnected and out of place. I wanted so badly to tell Sue who I really was and where I came from, but I knew that the minute I did, she'd ditch me and I'd have no idea what to do. This wasn't my time or my place and I was beginning to lose all hope of finding Ryn and getting home.

When we finally arrived in Tucson, my fingernails were so black that the dirt had made its way into my skin. A layer of sweat never left my body and my hair felt stiff and sticky. My lightweight dress, once clean and bright, looked like an old washcloth. Sue didn't look much better, but somehow, when she pulled her long brown hair up and rubbed her cheeks, no one would bother to look at what she was wearing.

Our last hitch dropped us off in downtown Tucson on a street corner next to a movie theater. Across from us was a telegraph office, a fur salon and a building that said "Loans." I stood there exhausted and lost, unlike my counterpart who seemed to get energized with every new experience.

"Aeden, you're not a lost sheep for heaven sakes, snap out of it. We've got to use our money to buy some new clothes and find a place to stay. We can't walk into the assayers office without an address and looking like Dickens' characters."

"Dickens?"

"Don't you read? Charles Dickens. You know, *Oliver Twist, David Copperfield, A Tale of Two ...*"

My mind jolted me back. And while I had never read any of Dickens' books, I did see "A Christmas Carol" on T.V. and the musical "Oliver." I nodded as Sue continued.

"First we'll go into a department store. This is a big enough city. It's bound to have a Filene's or Bloomingdales or even Macy's."

I gasped. Macy's? Back then? Sue was still talking, oblivious to my reaction.

"We'll find the ladies room, wash up and then purchase new dresses and if we have enough money, shoes and socks. Once we look decent, we'll find a room to let and have a real address."

"Rooms to let?"

"Yeah, to let, to rent, you know, they'll rent them for a few days or weeks."

My eyes darted across the street to the telegraph office and I thought about how we could try to find Ryn. But I knew that we needed an address before any ads or even telegraphs could be sent.

It wasn't very hard to find a department store. Sue asked the first person she saw on the street and within minutes we had washed our faces and arms and were trying on skirts and tops, only they were called "blouses." The skirts were dark and hung between our knees and ankles. The tops were in lighter colors and kind of billowy. Enough money for some awful looking plain shoes and socks. There was no way I was going to wear old fashioned stockings. Even Sue thought they'd be uncomfortable.

"Well, Aeden, what do you think? We look really respectable!"

"I guess."

"Are these your first new clothes? I honestly can't remember anything new I've worn until today. Everything came from the orphanage."

Sue insisted that we keep our old smelly clothes, just in case.

"We'll wash them once we get settled. We shouldn't throw anything away."

"Now what do we do?" I asked as we opened the large glass doors to the street.

"We start to find a place to live. Best bet is to sit down at a soda fountain and ask around. People will know what places are safe and which ones we should avoid."

Funny how she seemed to trust strangers, but her instincts were right. By late afternoon we rented a small room above a bakery. The bathroom was in the hallway and we had to share it with the other tenants. Our room had a small sink and an even smaller stove that I swore I'd never use if my life depended upon it. There was a single bed, couch, tiny table and two chairs.

A faded floral curtain framed the small window that overlooked the street.

"This is temporary," I kept whispering to myself. "Temporary."

But I felt like screaming and crying all at once. I missed my home, my family and my own reality. I tried not to let those strangling dark thoughts into my head, but honestly, I didn't know how much longer I could live in this decade without totally falling to pieces. But that wasn't the only thing that worried me.

Sure, we had earned some money from working at the mines, but it wasn't enough for new clothes, rent and the bit of food we ate. So where was Sue's money coming from? If she could steal a dead man's sock of gold, what other sinister things did she do? And worse yet, what was I capable of doing?

Chapter Eighteen:

Pete Holm

Pete Holm pushed open the rickety door to the cabin porch and took a step toward the boy. He had had second thoughts during the entire trek to the cabin but it was too late to change his course of action. Besides, they needed the boy. They needed someone who could go unnoticed. Someone who wouldn't arouse suspicion. But most of all, someone who wouldn't talk.

That boy wanted out of Morenci more than Pete did. But would the kid's old man come looking for him? Pete didn't think so. He cleared his throat and looked directly at Ryn.

"Looked like you were in an awful hurry to get away from your old man. What did you do to make him come after you with a shotgun?"

"He's not my father. And I didn't do anything."

"It sure didn't look that way from my angle."

"Well, I'm not his son, if that's what you're asking. But he thinks I'm his property."

"That so?"

"Yeah. And I'm not the only one. Lots of boys, and girls for that matter, were on a train. Next thing I know, I was sold as if I were a slave. Aren't there laws against this?"

Pete took a slow breath and chuckled to himself.

"So that's why you had no idea how to ride a horse. You're an orphan from back east. Is that it?"

"I suppose."

"And what about that talk of trying to find your sister? Were you just making up lies or was she on the train too?"

"Her name is Aeden. A E D E N. And I wasn't making it up."

"If she was on that train, there's no telling where she might be. And I'm not about to take you back to Morenci. Not now anyway. We've got business in Tucson and you're going to join us. No questions asked."

Pete slapped his hand on the gun that hugged his waist before continuing.

"Look, kid, no one's going to hurt you. But until we complete our business in Tucson, you need to be glued to us like stink on a skunk and do as we say. Tomorrow morning we'll be riding to Wilcox so I suggest you spend a little time getting acquainted with a saddle. You'll have your own horse."

Ryn swallowed the saliva that was building in his mouth and listened intently.

"There's some bread, peanut butter, milk and beef jerky inside. Might as well have a bite to eat. Come on, I'll introduce you to the men. So, what's your name?"

"Ryn"

"Rin? Like the dog? Rin Tin Tin?"

"Who? What dog?"

"Never mind. You probably never did see any movies being an orphan and all... Rin Tin Tin's a German Shepherd. Kept Warner Brothers Studios from bankruptcy. Never mind. Just go inside and eat."

Ryn started to open the door, then turned and faced the man.

"So what do I call you?"

"Name's Pete Holm. You can call me Mr. Pete to my face. Anything else I better not hear."

"Okay, Mr. Pete."

"The men inside are Bill and Hadley. And I suggest you call them mister, too."

Ryn turned and walked inside. He glanced backwards to see Mr. Pete sit on one of the wooden steps. But what he didn't see was the anguish and worry on Pete Holm's face. The conversation with Bill and Hadley hadn't gone that well, but there was no choice. The kid was going to be with them for a while, and had best not be a liability.

Chapter Nineteen:

Aeden

I watched as Sue opened a small tin of crackers and held them out for me to eat.

"Tomorrow morning we're going to walk into the assayers office with the gold and a letter from our father. We have to make this look legitimate. Then, we open a bank account and try not to call too much attention to ourselves."

"We don't have a letter. So how will anyone believe we have a father who gave us this gold?"

"Because we have paper and a fountain pen. In a few minutes, we'll have a letter."

I guess clothing wasn't the only thing that girl bought. She walked over to her rag-bag and pulled out a folded piece of paper, a thin pen and a tiny bottle of liquid. Then, she unscrewed the top of the pen and slowly poured the liquid in. All the while, I kept asking myself, "What year is this?"

"We need to think of an address, one that no one will question. And a name. A common name that no one can trace."

"What about Smith or Jones?"

"Too common. They'll know it's fake. Say, I have an idea. What about Greenway? Isabella Greenway is some hotsy-totsy Democrat around these parts. I read that somewhere. That name will probably just slip by."

"Okay. So what's our father's name?"

"Pick one."

"Frank. Frank Greenway. Let's make it even more impressive. Franklin. Like the president, Franklin Roosevelt."

"You mean Theodore?"

I gulped. FDR wouldn't be president for years, but Teddy Roosevelt was president a while back.

"Yeah, Theodore. That's what I meant."

"I like Franklin better. But I like Theodore, too. So, let's call our father Franklin Theodore Greenway."

"It sounds good."

"What about the address? We need to pick a city that's big enough so they won't be able to trace him."

"Pick the biggest one."

"Phoenix. We'll just use Phoenix."

"Now that we've agreed on the name and address, we need to write a very convincing letter."

Forget first drafts. Forget computers. Heck, we didn't even have an eraser. Our first copy had to be our final copy. I cringed as Sue put the pen on the paper and began to write. It seemed to take forever, but I've got to admit, it would fool anyone. It had to.

Chapter Twenty:

Ryn

*I*t's like I'm in some stinkin' lousy Western movie! I'm supposed to figure out how to ride a horse before morning? These guys are insane! Of course what do you expect with murderers? The peanut butter was soft and greasy and the bread was hard, but hey, it was food. I washed it down with some hot coffee. Black. Even though Bill and Hadley kept insisting that I put some milk in it.

"Coffee tastes like tar, kid. Just drink the milk."

"It's fine."

"You'd better get over to the lean-to and figure out how to saddle a horse. When you're done, come on back. I'll show you how to put on the reins. Then you can practice mounting and walking. We head out early in the day and this ain't no riding school."

There were four horses. The one we rode to get here, a plain greyish looking one with a black mane, and two brown horses with white blazes. They all looked enormous. I stood there for a while trying to decide which one wouldn't rear up in the air and toss me off. It didn't matter. They were all kind of scary. I mean, it's not like I'm a coward or anything. But there's a real difference when you're in control of something, like a skateboard or a bike, and when the thing you're riding has a mind of its own. I decided to have the upper hand.

"I'm in control," I announced as I dragged the heaviest saddle over to the greyish horse. It looked at me with a combination of curiosity and contempt.

The saddle must've weighed a ton! I don't know how I did it, but I did manage to throw it on the horse's back on my first try. Then I realized that it had to be fastened underneath. Crap! When I went to pull it, the damn thing fell off. Then the horse kept walking away from me as soon as I got close to it. A nightmare! A crummy, crappy Western nightmare!

It took me at least half a dozen tries, but I finally got it. Boy, talk about learning the hard way! I left the horse in its stall area and went to find Bill or Hadley. I had no intention of sticking my hands into a horse's mouth and trying to figure out how to attach the reins. I never thought I'd hear myself saying what I said, but I did.

"I need some instruction! Someone needs to teach me how to do this!"

"Calm down, kid," Hadley laughed when he saw how frustrated I was. "Come on, I'll give you a hand."

By the time the stars had started to show up in the sky, I had learned how to saddle a horse, mount it, and put on its reins. And, I learned how to take that stuff off, too. It's not like I was expecting any praise or anything, but when Hadley told me that I had done a decent job, I actually felt a sense of relief and pride. My fear was replaced with exhaustion. That was a good thing, because I dropped right off to sleep in a small cot near the cabin window. Thankfully, I never heard the conversation that took place late that night or I would never have slept again.

Chapter Twenty-one:

Pete Holm

Ryn was fast asleep on the small cot when Pete motioned for Bill and Hadley to step outside the cabin. He took a quick glance at the kid before shutting the door and speaking.

"Think he'll manage on the trail tomorrow? I mean it's pretty clear that the kid's never been around a horse or had to do any kind of manual work. From what I gather, and it's not much, he's probably just been on the streets back east."

Hadley sat on the narrow railing and leaned back.

"Kid seemed pretty determined to saddle the horse. And he caught on right away about the reins."

"Doesn't mean anything if the kid can't keep up," Bill stated coldly, his eyes locking with

Pete's. "And I just don't understand why on earth you brought him here to begin with."

"Like I said earlier, I didn't have any choice. His old man was out there with a shotgun and the miners were showing up. We couldn't risk having the kid talk. Besides, we need a runner. Someone no one will recognize. Someone who can move messages in and around Tucson without so much as raising an eyebrow."

"This isn't like you, Pete. I mean, bringing a young kid into this," Hadley said as he pushed the hair back from his face.

"You think I like doing this? But it may be our only opportunity."

"The kid's scared to death of you, you know. You can see it on his face."

"I know what he thinks and it's just as well. A little fear makes for a lot of obedience. Look, as soon as this is over, we'll..."

"We'll what?" Hadley grumbled. "Send him back to his old man so he can get the crap beaten out of him? Or maybe put him on another train back east? Man, you got us into some mess, Pete."

"So what do you suggest?"

"I don't know. But I'll think of something when we're done in Tucson."

"Enough said. We'd better get some sleep. We've got an early start. And for heaven sakes, find that kid an old pair of boots. We've got lots of them in the cabin. I don't know what kind of flimsy fancy-dancy shoes they wear back where he comes from, but he'll never make the ride with those things on."

Chapter Twenty-Two:

Aeden

Sue started to put the pen on the paper, then stopped and looked at me.

"How's your cursive?"

"My what?"

"Your cursive writing. Your script. How is it? I mean, if it's more polished than mine, maybe you should be the one writing the letter."

I gulped. Truth was I never learned script, or cursive, or whatever you call it. I just print and use a computer. Someday maybe an iPad2. But cursive? Who uses cursive in the 21st century? But then I remembered. This wasn't the 21st century.

"My cursive is terrible. That's what all my teachers told me. You'd better do the writing."

Sue shrugged and slowly started on the letter. An hour later we were looking at a genuine masterpiece of deceit, style, and finesse. I smiled as I read it out loud.

Franklin T. Greenway
Phoenix, Arizona
April 5, 1930

To Whom It May Concern:

I have entrusted my two daughters, Aeden and Sue Greenway, with this correspondence as my business obligations keep me from conducting this transaction in person. As the owner of a few small mines in the east, I wish to have the sample ore that my daughters have brought to your office processed to determine its gold balance and subsequent value. They have been directed to sell the ore for its market value and open a bank account in their names.

I trust that you will be able to handle this matter with utmost diligence and integrity as per your reputation.

My daughters have been directed to mail me a copy of their newly opened bank account statement so there will be no further need on your part, other than the initial transaction.

Please accept my gratitude for your prompt attention to this matter.

Sincerely,

Franklin T. Greenway

"So who's going to sign it?" I asked.

"Well, if your writing is as bad as you say it is, it might just work for the signature. I mean, we don't want it to look too fake."

I never forged a signature in my life. Not to get out of a class, not to hand in late homework, not for anything. But I've seen Ryn do it lots of times. Especially when he wanted to get out of something. "You're such a *goody-two shoes*" he'd tell me. Then he'd laugh it off. I knew Sue and I had to get away with this. I needed the money to start putting ads in the papers so I could find him and maybe find my way back. I took the pen from her hand, and, trying not to shake, created a signature that I knew I could replicate if it came down to that.

"Looks real to me, Aeden!"

"Let's hope it looks real enough to them."

"Stop worrying, Mrs. Grundy."

"Who's Mrs. Grundy?"

"It's an expression. I swear Aeden, sometimes I think you're from another planet all together."

I started to stammer.

"It's, it's...it's just that I..."

"Don't worry. I won't tell," Sue winked, as she carefully placed the letter off to the side of the table and cleared away the pen.

For a moment, I wanted to tell her everything. Tell her who I really was and how desperately I needed to get home. But I couldn't take that chance. Not yet. And maybe not ever.

Chapter Twenty-Three:

Ryn

My toes felt like they were in a vise and I swear I couldn't wiggle them if I tried. But Hadley insisted that I wear these stinky old cowboy boots.

"You go traipsing in the brush to do your business and next thing you know a rattler bites your ankle. Yep, put on those boots. You'll thank me later."

I just grimaced.

We were up before the sunrise and next thing I knew I was putting a saddle on the grey horse from yesterday. Someone did me a favor and the reins were already in the horse's mouth. I used the horn of the saddle as a hook to tie my sneakers so I could take them with me. I had every intention of putting them back on the minute we got to wherever we were going.

I watched as the men crammed all sorts of stuff into the saddle bags and filled canteens with water. Next thing I knew, I was directed to ride in between Bill and Hadley with Mr. Pete at the lead.

For the first hour I kept trying to figure out if these were any famous murderers from history like John Dillinger or Machine Gun Kelly, but no one with names like Pete, Hadley or Bill came to mind. Still…a killer is a killer and I wasn't about to mess with any of them. I figured that I might have a chance of slipping away once we got to civilization. Then, I'd do whatever I could to find Aeden. I kept telling myself that she was okay, because I didn't want to think otherwise.

Don't ask me where the heck we were going because I didn't have a clue. All I knew was that we were riding uphill for most of the time on narrow trails. Compared to Oregon, these were small mountains, but they were mountains and going uphill meant one thing. We'd have to come down eventually.

My butt stuck to the saddle like an insect on flypaper. The only relief I had was when we'd stop every now and then to give the horses a break and take a drink of metallic-tasting water from one of the canteens. I swear on my life that if my family ever decides to spend a vacation on a dude ranch, I'll bolt out of there screaming for my life!

My companions, if you could call them that, were none too talkative. At least not around me. And I didn't say much either. I just let my horse do the walking as we threaded through scrub brush and pine trees. The higher we got, the more scraggly the pines. Nope, this sure wasn't Oregon.

Mr. Pete's voice broke the silence as we continued to climb.

"We'll camp at Turkey Flat. Shouldn't be too much longer."

"Is that a city?" I asked.

But there was no need for a reply. Everyone started to laugh before Hadley spoke.

"Turkey Flat is as much of a city like this here piece of jerky is prime rib!"

I rolled my eyes and continued to stare at the terrain. In the distance, mountains looked bigger. Green. Blue. Pink. We were climbing all right. I only hoped that it would be a slow descent down from Turkey Flat. And to where? I couldn't even begin to guess.

My butt was now numb. Raw and numb. Any longer on this trail and I would have fallen off the damn horse. I couldn't even feel where my body connected to the saddle. So when we finally reached a large clearing at the top of who-knows-what mountain I started looking around for some sort of civilization, figuring this must be Turkey Flat.

"Is this it?" I yelled to Hadley.

"Yeah, kid. This is Turkey Flat."

I could see a large pond in the distance and a few primitive cabins. Hadley was right about the place.

"Are we going to stay here long?"

"Long as it takes; now be quiet and keep moving."

The cabins looked closer than they actually were and it seemed to take forever till we reached the furthest one and got off our horses. Mr. Pete wasted no time barking orders.

"Okay, Rin Tin Tin, you and Hadley go water the horses. I've got business inside."

I watched as he and Bill walked into the cabin. From the looks of it, housekeeping was the last thing on anyone's mind. Lots of broken boards, a few empty bottles, and some old cans littered the front yard. Then I saw a tall, muscular guy step outside and shake Mr. Pete's hand. Great. Probably another murderer. A few more days and we could hold a regular convention. I didn't say anything as Hadley and I lead the four horses to the pond.

More than anything, I wished I could have heard their conversation, but Mr. Pete closed the door quickly as he and the guy went inside. It wasn't until much later that I found out who he was. Well, at least his name, anyway. Like I said, Mr. Pete wasn't big on conversation.

"This is Halloway. He'll be joining us tomorrow when we head to Wilcox. We'll be leaving the horses with him when we get there. Got a car waiting. Shouldn't take but a day or so to make it to Tucson. That is if we don't break down."

Everyone chuckled except me. I mean what on earth was so funny about having your car break down. Unless of course they were used to it. Really used to it.

Another lousy night sleeping on an old cot. Impossible to get comfortable. But I figured that if I pretended to be asleep, I could hear what they were saying and maybe figure out what they were planning. Geez, I hoped it wasn't another murder in Tucson. Hearing one guy get shot was enough for me.

I heard them talking, all right. But nothing they said made sense. At least not at that time.

"Dead?"

"Yeah."

"And the paper?"

"No."

"Wasn't stashed with the gold?"

"No time to look."

"So, it's still out there."

"Fraid so."

"You know what this means."

"Yeah. Better make sure we have lots of bullets when we get to Tucson."

Gold? Bullets? Dead? That should've served me right for trying to listen in on the conversation. It was one hell of bedtime story. One I should not have listened to. Still, I couldn't help myself.

"What about the kid?

"Don't worry. We'll take care of him when all of this is over."

My hands began to shake. Good thing they were under the lightweight sheet Hadley gave me. I kept my eyes closed and tried to even out my breathing. All I had to do was get to Tucson. From there I could make a run for it and try to find Aeden. If I lived that long.

Chapter Twenty-Four:

Aeden

A re you just going to walk into the office with the letter and that old sock?"

Sue paused from combing her long, dark hair and looked my way.

"You're right. We shouldn't be carrying the gold in this crummy sock. We'd better put it into something else. What about a handkerchief? "

"A what?"

"A handkerchief. Didn't you hear me? I've got a couple of fancy ones stashed away with my things."

The minute I saw Sue return with a lacy white piece of linen, I recognized it immediately. Guess they didn't have tissues back then. She unfolded the sock and let the gold nuggets drop onto her bed. Then she gave the sock another shake, and that's when a small piece of paper fell out.

"Oh my gosh," she said. "I didn't know anything else was in with the gold."

"What does it say?"

"See for yourself. There's nothing written on the paper, just the indentations from another letter. This piece of paper must have been underneath it. The markings are very faint but the gold dust kind of outlines some of it."

"Get a pencil," I shouted, "and we can rub over the indents to see what was on the paper."

"Great idea!"

I watched as Sue rubbed the lead over the paper, waiting for a response. But she just stood there looking and thinking.

"Well, what is it?"

"Longitude and latitude lines and a series of numbers with dashes in-between."

I looked down and saw what she was talking about. The first line made sense. Well, it would have made sense if we had a map of the world. The second line looked vaguely familiar. If the numbers had been in a group of three, I would have figured it was a locker combination. But these numbers formed a group of five. Then, it dawned on me. It was a combination all right, but not to a locker. The combination was to a safe or a vault. Like the kind you'd find in the home of some really wealthy person.

32° 13' 18"N / 110° 55' 32"W

16-18-9-19-13

I picked up the paper to take a closer look, holding it to the light. I could see longer indentations on the bottom of the page, but without tracing over it with the pencil, it was impossible to make out.

"Keep rubbing the lead on the paper, Sue. There's more."

Her wrist moved furiously across the page. Then I heard a short gasp.

"What? What does it say?"

Sue spoke slowly and deliberately, emphasizing each word.

"Helene and Mabel Pearsall"

"This is a combination meant for them, whoever they are. And maybe the gold was meant for them, too. I just don't feel right about any of this. Now what do we do?"

Sue's eyes widened as she took another look. Then she put the paper back in the sock and placed it under the mattress.

"We don't even know who they are, or if they have anything to do with the note. I mean, their names were on another paper and just formed an indentation. We don't have time to find out right now. We really need to take the gold to the assayer. It's not safe leaving it here much longer."

"I know. But what if the numbers lead us to more money? More money that's not ours."

"Then we'd better get lots of deposit slips!"

"I'm serious, Sue. It's not our money. Not really."

"Then whose? Some dead man's? Some women named Helene and Mabel? Come on, Aeden, when we're filthy rich you can make a donation to your favorite charity. Mine is starting right here. Now hurry up!"

"It just feels wrong."

"Tell you what, Aeden, we'll see if we can figure out who Helene and Mabel are, but first things first. And it doesn't mean we're giving them our money. For all we know, Helene and Mabel are someone's cleaning ladies. And whatever you do, don't act guilty or scared when we walk into the assayer's office. You can be so mousey at times!"

"Mousey?"

"You know, scared and shy. Time to stand up and take what's ours, even if we didn't exactly come by it on the up and up. Still, finders keepers, losers weepers."

I didn't bother to say anything else.

A few minutes later, we walked into the assayer's office the way we had practiced for days. Heads up and confident. I let Sue do the talking when a round-faced middle aged gentleman wearing glasses approached us.

"We are Sue and Aeden Greenway. This letter from our father should explain our intent."

The man took the letter and walked over to a small desk. I tried not to show any emotion as I watched him read it.

"Your father does not mention the name of the mines."

"Does that matter?" Sue's voice was cold and unassuming.

"No, I suppose not. Well, let's measure and determine your sample."

Sue opened her white handkerchief and dropped the contents into a small bowl. Her eyes never left the gold as she watched the man wrap it in foil and place it in some sort of an oven.

"Process is going to take a while. You're welcome to wait, or you could come back later."

"We'll wait right here," Sue said as she motioned me to some small wooden benches off to the side of the room.

The man was right when he said the process would take a while. Other assayers were helping miners with silver and copper. For some reason, that process was less time consuming. Finally, after what seemed like hours, the man approached us.

"Are you sure you don't know what mine this came from?"

"Our father did not say, but I trust the gold content is strong."

"Strong? Why, yes. It's quite strong. In fact, it's about the purest one can find."

Sue tried not to show any emotion as the man continued. I bit my lower lip and held my breath.

"Your sample weighs in at 28 troy ounces. At the given rate of $20.65 per ounce, you'd been looking at a stately sum of $578.20."

While that amount of money was decent in my time, I imagined that it was probably half someone's yearly salary in 1930. I held still.

"As my father directed, we shall need to sell you the ore and open a bank account."

The man nodded. "To whom do I write this check?"

Fifteen minutes later, we were standing on a cold marble floor inside Tucson's largest bank. And when our transaction was finally complete, we left with a small register book inside a brand new leather case. The opening line read:

> Opening Balance = $578.20
> Then today's transaction:

Withdrawal = -5.00
Balance =$573. 20

Once outside, Sue handed me $2.50 and smiled.

"You can place your ad now, Aeden. Newspaper office is right down the street. Then we're off to the library."

"The library?"

"Where else are we going to figure out what those longitude and latitude lines mean?"

"But you left them under your mattress."

"No, I also left them in my brain, now come on!"

As we rounded the corner, I caught a glimpse of the daily paper. It was stacked up in front of a newsstand. Sue saw it, too and we both froze.

MINE OWNER MURDERED IN MORENCI
SHERIFF'S INVESTIGATION TURNS
STATEWIDE

Chapter Twenty-Five:

Ryn

I got up the next morning on my own. Early. No one shaking me or yelling at me. At least no one in Mr. Pete's "Merry Mob of Murderers." I got up while it was still dark because I felt something crawl down the front of my chest. Found out later it was a tick. A tick!

My skin was so dirty and crummy and stinky that it was now the perfect home for ticks and fleas and whatever godforsaken bugs were in this state. And if that wasn't bad enough, a layer of sweat had adhered to my entire body. I stunk! Days of sweating and riding with no shower and no clean clothes left a nasty stench on me. No wonder a tick was on my chest. Probably looking for a place to call home.

Unlike the other spot, we had to use the pond for water. It was still dark when I returned to the cabin from washing my face and most of my arms. Someone had heated up coffee and it looked as if everyone was in a hurry. Mr. Pete gave the orders like a drill sergeant.

"Hadley and Bill, get the horses ready. Don't just stand there Rin, help them!"

I didn't wait to be told again. I bolted for the lean-to and got busy real quick with the saddles. No time for conversation. We were on the trail to Wilcox before the sun had even broken through the horizon.

"I figure we'll have one night of camping just below Bonita, before we make it to Wilcox," Hadley said as he turned to face me. Our horses were side by side for just a brief second before the trail narrowed. Hadley continued, "Trail gets steep and rocky. Just stay alert and whatever you do, don't lean forward or shift your weight. Got it?"

"Sure," I said.

I was in the middle of the line with Halloway and Bill behind me. Guess they figured someone needed to keep an eye on me. I didn't complain.

Hadley wasn't kidding when he said the trail gets steeper as we go. At times it looked as if we'd plunge to our deaths. I just prayed under my breath that my horse would keep its balance. The only good thing about the ride was the fact that I was so freaking scared, that I didn't have time to think about my sister and worry. I mean, it's not that Aeden isn't smart or resourceful, but still…she's my younger sister and I do feel responsible.

After what seemed like hours of nail biting, white knuckle squeezing, holding on for dear life riding, we reached a spot where the trail widened and the pitch wasn't so steep. As usual, Mr. Pete gave the orders.

"Rest the horses. Water up ahead."

My body felt beaten and bruised from the ride. I didn't think my horse was too thrilled either. As Hadley and I walked the animals to a small brook, Bill approached with his horse in tow.

"Couple of hours more and we'll be there. Boy, sitting pretty in that Tin-Lizzy is going to feel awfully good!"

I had to think for a moment. I remembered that expression from a project my 6th grade class did on the 1920s. "Tin-Lizzy." It was a car. Some sort of car. Maybe a Ford. I looked at Bill and spoke.

"Are we all going to ride in it? I mean, will it hold all of us?"

"Don't know what Mr. Pete told you, but yeah, the car holds four or five. Just don't know if you're one of them."

"Don't scare the kid," Hadley said. Then he turned to me.

"Stop worrying. We're not leaving you on the side of a road or anything."

"I'm not worried."

Actually, I wished they would have left me on the side of a road. A big, well-trafficked road that led to a populated city. It would have been better than what they probably intended to do with me.

I bent down to take a closer look at the newspaper. A newsboy was standing guard over them and didn't look too pleased.

"This ain't no lending library. It'll cost ya five cents if you want a copy."

"We do," Sue replied before I could say anything.

We walked quickly to the side of a building and read the story ourselves. Sure enough, the mine owner was shot and killed inside the mine. It was definitely the dead guy we saw. The dead guy whose gold we took. According to the article, "the Greenlee County Sheriff's Office has requested assistance from the U.S. Marshals to track the killer."

I went nuts. Scared stiff. It was bad enough that I was lost in another time without my brother, but now I was probably being hunted by the police.

"Calm down, Aeden. You're going to give me the Heebie-jeebies. We didn't kill the guy. We're not the murderers. They are not looking for us!"

"How do you know? We're the ones with his gold."

"Didn't you read the whole thing? The article says they're looking for some gang that may be responsible. Apparently these guys are brutal. Would shoot anyone on a dime."

Then she looked at the expression on my face before she continued.

"Relax, Aeden, they're not after us! Maybe you'll stop being so scared once you find your brother."

I felt the two dollars and two quarters in the small pocket of my skirt.

"Where did you say the newspaper office was?"

"Just down the street. Let's go. If you place the ad now, it will probably start with tomorrow's paper."

I kept it short and to the point. I only wanted Ryn to see it and respond.

Twelve year old sister seeks
Lost brother
In AZ.
Time to come home. Remember your note.
Leave message at telegraph office in
response to this ad.

"You sure you want it spaced like that, miss?"

"Yes. Just like that."

"And you want it going out in all of our syndicated papers?"

"Yes."

"It will cost you $1.75 for the week."

I paid the gentleman and held on to my remaining 75 cents as if were a small fortune. Wherever Ryn was, he was sure to see the ad and figure it out. I mean, it wouldn't take a rocket scientist to break the code. A three year old could do it. But it would only make sense to Ryn, and maybe, just maybe, that was the case with our other code, the one with the longitude and latitude. Perhaps it was only supposed to make sense to someone in particular. But that wasn't the case.

It was a short walk to 6th Street and the library. Funny how those old buildings all seem to look the same— imposing columns, broad steps, and no warmth. Inside was no different.

I was petrified to even make a sound as I walked across the floor. Two older women were seated at a large front desk with a card catalog behind them. I'd seen pictures of card catalogs but never the real thing. All I had to do was use a computer or push an app to find a book or DVD. I had no idea how to use a card catalog but I knew Sue did. In any case, it didn't matter because what we needed was directly in front of us—a large globe on a stand.

Sue put her index finger to her lip to tell me to keep quiet. She didn't have to. I had no intention of talking. Then she whispered, "Take a look. We just have to connect the numbers."

Her fingers spun the globe and I watched. Then she poked me in the arm and all but yelled, "If this isn't copacetic, I don't know what is!"

"What is what? What's copacetic? What place?"

"Tucson! The longitude and latitude point to Tucson! That's what makes it so great, so wonderful...so copacetic! We're here! We don't have to go anywhere but here!"

"Okay," I said as I moved closer to the globe. "So, what we're looking for is a safe or a vault in Tucson. That's hardly enough information."

"Maybe not, but there's something else. The names. Helene and Mabel Pearsall. Those names must mean something."

"Yeah. The two women whose gold we have."

"We don't know that. All we have is information that may or may not have come from the dead mine owner. After all, I found it on a ledge. It wasn't as if I dug through his pockets or anything."

"So who do you suppose Helene and Mabel Pearsall are? His daughters?"

"Only one way to find out. We'll ask the librarian to help us."

Sue turned away from the globe and headed directly to the information desk. A thin woman in her 30's or early 40's was busy stamping books. The two older women were no longer in front of the card catalog.

"Excuse me," Sue whispered. "Do you know how we can locate two people who live in Tucson?"

"We have telephone directories for Tucson and Phoenix in the adjacent corridor."

Sue nodded and grabbed me by the arm.

Surprisingly, the phonebook didn't look that much different than the ones we get delivered to our door each fall, except that it was much narrower and very decorative on the front cover. An embellished design of an eagle in front of the American flag stood below the word "Tucson."

We immediately tried to find a listing for Pearsall, but there was nothing.

"What about Helene or Mabel? Would they list it under the first name?" I said.

"Not likely, but let's look."

Again, nothing. Well, not exactly nothing. There was a listing for H. Mabel on Pennington Street, but we were sure it had nothing to do with our letter.

Sue was determined.

"Maybe the librarian knows how to find these names if they've appeared in an article or even an obituary in the newspaper. I'm going back to ask her."

The lady was still stamping books when Sue returned.

"What did you say the names were?"

"Helene and Mabel Pearsall."

"Helene and Mabel Pearsall? You girls must not be from around here. Helene and Mabel Pearsall aren't people, well, let me correct that. They used to be residents decades ago. But Helene and Mabel Pearsall is a street corner. A prominent street corner in the old Victorian section of the city. Their former mansion sits on that corner. Or should I say, deteriorates on that corner? Seems no one could find a deed of transfer when they died or family members for that matter. So...the house just rots there. The city doesn't want to incur any expenses having to do with the place. So sad, really.

Their father was Herbert Pearsall, a financier and entrepreneur. The older sister, Helene died a spinster. But the younger one, Mabel, defied her father's demands and ran off with some man. They went east to New York or maybe Boston. Herbert Pearsall was never the same man after that. And Mabel never returned to Tucson. No one knows what became of them. But the streets were named after the girls."

Sue gave my ankle a quick kick and smiled before she continued her conversation with the librarian.

"Can you tell us how to get there?"

Minutes later we were following a sketchy map that the librarian had drawn with street names that we actually recognized. Broadway. Alameda. Church. Main. Sue all but ran to Helene and Mabel Pearsall.

"This is so exciting. My feet just can't move fast enough."

"Slow down," I said. "We don't even know what we'll find when we get there. Or...what we'll do for that matter."

"I know what we're going to do. We have a combination. We just need to find the safe!"

"I'm not breaking into some house or bank for that matter just because we have a combination to a safe. I mean, taking gold from a dead man was bad enough. This is…this is… this is the stuff that lands people in jail for crying out loud!"

"Look around you, Aeden. It's the Depression. Do you want to live your life just scrounging around or washing dirty pots? You need to toughen up and take some chances. Now come on."

More than anything, I wanted that ad to reach Ryn. I wanted him to make his way to Tucson and get us out of here. If anyone could figure out this whole time travel thing, it was him. I tried to conceal the fact that my lips were trembling and my hands were shaking, but I was no good at covering things up.

"Aeden, please. Let's just find the place. Then we can decide what to do. All right?"

I nodded in agreement, but I felt a knot in my stomach that twisted and pulled as we approached Helene and Mabel Pearsall. A knot that gripped me like a vise and wouldn't let go. I should have listened to the warning.

Chapter Twenty-Seven:

Ryn

*T*here was no cabin in Bonita. No barn. No lean-to. Nothing. Just lots of open space, a few small trees and the distant outline of mountains. The mountains I think we just came down. If I were planning a nice camping trip in a well-stocked RV, this would have been the place. But camping on the hard ground with even more bugs was obviously what Mr. Pete had in mind. They were skirting the authorities all right. And they picked a pretty good route. No one would come looking for them here. And by the time they got to their getaway car in Wilcox, the sheriff would be long gone.

"Rin!" someone yelled. "You know how to start a fire?"

"Sort of."

"Well start gathering some small pieces of wood and brush. We've got to deal with the horses and get some tents set up."

It was Bill's voice. Halloway, Hadley and Mr. Pete were already leading the horses to a small pond.

I looked up at Bill.

"Do we rub the pieces of wood together?"

"Haven't you heard of matches, kid?"

I watched as he took a small, colorful matchbook from his pocket and proceeded to strike the first match, holding it out for me to see.

"It's 1930, kid. Not the stone age."

I nodded and took a quick breath, trying to piece all of this together. 1930. So that's what year this is. I wasn't far off in my thinking. This was probably one of the last stops for that orphan train before the depression. The Great Depression. Stupid prisms. The Great Depression. I couldn't imagine a worse time in history, unless of course it was the Inquisition and that didn't happen in our country.

"Haven't you ever seen a campfire, kid?"

Bill's voice cut through my train of thought and I mumbled some sort of a response that he dismissed quickly before continuing.

"All you need to do, Rin-Tin, is add more small twigs to the fire and then start adding larger branches. You understand?"

"Yeah, I've got it."

"Got what?"

"I mean, I understand."

"Good. Because this fire is the only thing that's going to keep us warm tonight. So don't let it go out."

Bill wasn't kidding. It was a cold, moonless night and we threw whatever blankets we had over the makeshift sleeping bags. 1930. No thermo wear. Just old scratchy wool blankets. Still, it was better than freezing our butts off. Dinner was a real treat, too. More beef jerky and rock hard bread. Even Hadley complained. Enough to get Mr. Pete's attention.

"Quit grousing. There'll be a hot meal waiting for us in Wilcox."

Halloway broke off another piece of the bread and took a bite before spitting most of it out.

"Better be. Didn't exactly sign up for this."

I listened carefully as he and Mr. Pete carried the conversation.

"No one did. It just goes with the job, you know."

"So, you think anyone from Morenci is on to us?"

"No, but that's why we're keeping a distance. Don't want to raise a single eyebrow."

"What about Tucson? Anyone else coming?"

Good thing it was dark because my eyes just about bugged out of my head. What did he mean "anyone else coming?" What the heck was this? A murderers' convention?

"Couple of guys from Phoenix, just in case. We'll have to send a telegraph from Wilcox."

"So what did the note say?"

By now I was getting really good at pretending to be asleep. I stretched out, kept my eyes shut and listened.

"Only got half the note. It was ripped apart. Still, easy enough to figure out."

"Go on."

"Got the latitude, last 2 digits and a name. Mabel Pearsall."

"Latitude puts us on the direct line to Tucson."

"And Mabel Pearsall?"

"We'll find her."

"We may be running out of time."

"I know. Whoever's holding the other half of the note has most of the combination and enough info to figure out it's Tucson. Just means we can't dilly dally in Wilcox."

"Are we taking the kid?"

"Yeah. They won't suspect a kid."

"You know this could cost you your…"

"Shh… I know. Enough said. I'm getting some sleep."

My body felt tense and rigid. Sleep was the last thing I was worried about. And yeah, I must admit, while a hot meal in Wilcox sounded good, the thought of being used as bait for these guys made me even more determined to get the hell away as soon as I could.

*T*he house took up the entire corner lot, creating its own atmosphere. One that I didn't like. Ornate. Embellished. Overdone. That would have been all right if it had been occupied. But sitting vacant on the corner, it was intimidating, menacing and creepy. And while it wasn't exactly boarded up or overgrown with weeds and cobwebs, it still had the look of something whose life was sucked out of it years ago. I stood on the sidewalk motionless, while Sue approached the old black wrought iron fence that enclosed it. The garden, if you could call it that, was a mess of cactus, bougainvillea, sage and whatever other desert plant had made its way here to spread and die. I just wanted to get as far away from

Helene and Mabel Pearsall as possible. Sue, on the other hand, was mesmerized.

"Just look at this place, Aeden. Why, it's just inviting us to come inside!"

"I didn't hear any invitation. It's trespassing."

"Do you see any signs that say DO NOT ENTER?"

"No, but still… And besides, it's going to get dark pretty soon."

"We still have an hour or so. Let's just walk around and see if there's an open window or maybe a side door unlocked."

Both of us were pretty sure that the heavy wooden front door with its detailed panels was locked good and tight. We didn't even bother to check it out. Instead, we walked along all four sides of the house, looking for signs of an open window. My fear was starting to become noticeable.

"You don't really plan on crawling through some window. It'll be pitch dark in there."

"Let's just see if there's a way to get in. Then we'll come back early tomorrow. Broad daylight. Nothing for you to worry about."

"And all we're doing is going in there looking for a safe or vault?"

"That's right. That's all we have to do. Find the vault. Open it. And…"

"And steal something! Sue, I just don't think I can do this!"

"You don't even know what we're going to find. Besides, I don't think it belongs to anyone anymore."

"You mean the house or what we'll find?"

"Both. Now come on. Let's keep looking."

We crept around the entire building but there were no open windows. I could see that Sue was getting annoyed.

"We might just have to break a window, Aeden. We can break it today, and then come back early tomorrow. Might as well start looking around for a large rock or something."

"Trespassing is one thing. Breaking a window is another. It's breaking and entering!"

"Technically, it's just breaking. We haven't entered. Now will you please stop being such a goody-goody and help me find a rock?"

We were in the back yard, surrounded by dense brush. A few old terra cotta flower pots lined the side of the building.

"That big one will do," Sue said. "Just hand it to me."

Against my better judgment, or any judgment for that matter, I bent down and lifted the pot. It had been on the ground for so long that I actually had to pry it from the hard dirt. The air around it seemed to gasp as I lifted it up. It was then that I realized we wouldn't need to break a window after all.

"Oh, my gosh! There's an old key underneath the flowerpot! I bet it's where they kept the spare key to the front door!"

I dropped the pot at my feet, picked up the small key and walked quickly to the front door.

"I thought you were against breaking and entering," Sue said, as I waved the key in front of her.

"This is just entering. Entering with a key. No harm in that."

The key was old and rusty. I wiped it against my skirt until most of the rust fell off.

"The key's so old, I don't know if it'll still work."

"Just give it a try!"

Sue watched as I put the key into the only opening on the door. It fit all right, but it was so ancient that it could no longer work the assembly mechanism for the lock.

We both stood there, looking at the garden and getting more exasperated by the minute. Then Sue noticed something. Something she had read about.

"Aeden, look! Over there! It's Aloe vera plants."

"So what?"

"So when you break them off, they have a sticky liquid that people use for burns. Let's break one off and put the liquid on the key. It might just do the trick."

The liquid was gummy and thick but I made sure to coat every inch of that key before inserting it back into the doorknob hole. Slowly, carefully, I twisted the key. A quick click and the door gave way.

The smell of dust and stale air filled my nostrils as my eyes scanned the room. We were standing in a small foyer looking straight ahead at four piercing eyes and they seemed to be moving. The setting sun had cast its light on a portrait of two girls with deep brown eyes and long, dark curly hair. But the sunlight had passed through a heavy chandelier in the adjacent room, causing the painting to flicker and its subjects to move.

And while I stood frozen, fixed to the girls in the portrait, Sue walked over to the chandelier and reached up to touch one of its dangling prisms. She lingered there with the strangest look on her face before she finally spoke.

"No wonder the girls look as if they are alive. It's all in the refraction."

Chapter Twenty-Nine:
Ryn

The trail from Bonita to Wilcox wasn't as steep or harrowing as the one down from Morenci. Still, it wasn't exactly a pleasure ride. My feet felt glued to my boots and they probably were. Maybe Hadley was trying to scare the crap out of me with his stories of snakes and scorpions, and frankly, as much as I hate to admit it, he succeeded. No way were these boots coming off of me until I was indoors somewhere.

We moved across a large flatland that seemed to stretch forever. I later found out it was the Sulfur Springs Valley, not that it mattered because we didn't find any springs, just enough turkey vultures flying around to give me the creeps. And there wasn't much conversation either, just a few words here and there. And of course, Mr. Pete's orders.

"Better make sure the horses are watered and rested before we hit the next mountain range."

I figured they had some use for me or they would've gotten rid of me by now. No one would have found my body in the mountains, and if they did, most of it would have been a "happy meal" for the turkey vultures. Still, I had a plan. Well, not a detailed, elaborate plan, just a quick "get the hell out of here plan." I was going to enjoy whatever hot meal was waiting for us in Wilcox and take my chances with the ride to Tucson. I knew that I had a better chance of making an escape in a big city where it would be harder to find me.

I tried not to let my mind drift too much, but geez, it was so damn monotonous. The steady click of the horses' hooves, the slow rustling of the wind and the annoying bird calls would be enough to send even the most resolute person to madness. I couldn't believe it but I actually found myself wishing we could sing a stupid song or something. Then I remembered who I was riding with and songs were probably not in their repertoire.

We continued in sullen, stupid silence with the occasional break every now and then until it was almost dusk and the flatlands were behind us. Halloway was the first one to open his mouth and I all but jumped out of my saddle just to hear a voice.

"Looks like we're almost there. Just over this hill and we'll be at the house."

"Who's house?" I blurted out.

"It's a house we stay at when we've got business in this territory," Hadley replied.

"Shouldn't matter whose house it is," Mr. Pete said, "just mind your business."

I took that to mean that we were all done with our conversation and didn't make another sound until much later when we arrived at a small ranch house on the outskirts of Wilcox. Bill, Hadley and Halloway took the horses to a barn while I was directed by Mr. Pete to go inside.

"Miss Ida Mae keeps this place in order for us and will have a meal ready. You can go inside and introduce yourself but I wouldn't say too much if I were you."

"Name, rank, serial number, got it." I said.

"Don't try to be funny."

I watched as Mr. Pete joined the other men and could see that they were engaged in some sort of animated conversation. Certainly a hell of a lot more than what took place on our trek here.

Miss Ida Mae looked to be past middle aged but not old. Hard to say. Her brownish hair was tied up in a bun and she was wearing a blue and green floral dress that looked like something I might have seen in a book about the Amish people. But she wasn't Amish. At least I didn't think so. I must have startled her because the minute I walked in she jumped.

"I, I...wasn't expecting anyone except the regular gentlemen who stay here."

"I'm with them. I'm Ryn."

"Rin?"

"Yeah."

"Is that your given name or a nickname? Never mind. Not my business. You can wash up just down the hall. Dinner will be on the table in a few minutes."

Wash up. Soap and water. Who would have thought I'd be flipping out over using soap and water. I all but ran to the bathroom. Outside, the guys were still talking. Miss Ida Mae opened the front door, stepped outside and yelled for Mr. Pete. With the bathroom window opened, I could hear their conversation.

"You brought a young boy to this place? What's the matter with you?"

"Couldn't be helped, Ida. Believe me; I didn't plan it this way."

"Are you taking him to Tucson?"

"Uh huh."

"Won't his family be looking for him?"

"I don't think he has any."

"Well, think again. Today's paper arrived from Tucson and there's something in the personal ads you might just want to look at."

Chapter Thirty:
Aeden

“It’s going to be dark soon, Sue. I really think we should be getting out of here.”

“Aren’t you the least bit curious?”

If I had to choose between fear and curiosity, fear was certainly the winner. The house was stuffy and dusty, the perfect combination for an allergy attack. But that wasn’t what bothered me. I had the most awful sense that we were being watched. I knew it was just my imagination, but as the sun began to set, all sorts of weird shadows seemed to pop up from nowhere.

"We won't be able to find anything in the dark anyway, so we might as well go back to our place."

"Let's just take a quick look downstairs. Then we'll lock the place up and be back in the morning."

"You're sounding as if it's your place."

"Right now it is. I don't see anyone else making a grand entrance."

With that, she left the foyer and headed down a narrow hallway. I just stood still listening to her.

"Nothing here. Just a pantry, kitchen, lots of hanging pots and pans and some sort of built in cabinet for the china."

"Hurry-up!"

"Whoa, really classy living room, Aeden. Just take a peek."

She wasn't kidding. If it weren't for the fact that the heavy red curtains looked as if they could disintegrate at any second, or the furniture might be consumed by termites, it would have rivaled an historical museum.

"Okay. I've seen it. Now can we go?"

"Where do think they would have put the vault?"

I knew Sue wasn't about to leave without at least locating the one thing we came here for, even if it meant we'd wind up walking home in pitch darkness.

"Vaults are really heavy so I doubt it would be upstairs."

"I agree. It'll only take us a few more minutes, Aeden. I'll check out the rooms to the right and you can walk around by the dining room."

I didn't feel like arguing. I just wanted to get this over with, so I moved out of the foyer and into a large dining area. The archway that separated both rooms was framed in the most detailed carved wood I'd ever seen. In fact, once I took a good look, I could see that all the archways downstairs had the same intricate wooden carvings. Embossed, round spindles with leaves and acorns. Odd for the southwest.

The dining room table was enormous; and I'm sure that underneath the layer of red dust that coated it, was some sort of expensive wood. Two wingback chairs were the sentinels that guarded either end of the table, watching over the smaller armless chairs. Against the wall was a gigantic sideboard with old serving trays and bowls on the center shelves. They, too, were covered in red dust. On either side were fancy doors with more carvings. This time trees, birds and deer.

I could see that both of the doors had small keyholes. Still, I gave one of them a pull just in case it wasn't locked. It didn't budge. Same with the other one. Then I thought for a moment. "If I had a locking hutch or cabinet, I'd want the key nearby so I wouldn't have to go all over the place to get it. But…I'd want it tucked away so no one else would find it." And that's when I realized that the key must be in one of the bowls on the middle shelf. High enough for an adult to reach, but not so high that they would need a chair. Unfortunately, I did need a chair and those old dining room ones looked as if they'd break apart if I tried to stand on them. But the small table in the corner of the room looked sturdy enough.

While Sue was checking out the rest of the house, I lifted the lid of an oval serving bowl and looked inside. I was right! A tiny skeleton key had been there long enough to leave a dusty imprint of itself, even though the lid was on. I lifted it gingerly and put it in my pocket for tomorrow's "find." Sue would never leave the house if she thought that the vault was behind one of those doors and the key was in our hands. My secret would keep for another day.

It was one thing snooping around a dusty, creepy old house in daylight. Ryn and I were getting plenty of practice at great Auntie Zanne's. But it was another thing at night. So, I returned the table to its place in the corner and walked out of the room as if nothing had happened.

The sunbeam from the chandelier prisms had long left the parlor and was no longer illuminating the portrait of the two girls. Still, their features were easily discernible. Both had dark brown eyes, thick lashes and long, curly hair. The shorter one had two dimples and a small beauty mark near the corner of an eye. If it weren't the most preposterous thought in the world, I could have sworn that there was a third sister, one who was absent from the painting, but not the house. I'm surprised she didn't see it for herself. Too busy looking for gold or clues or whatever else was going on in Sue's mind. But it was obvious to me. She looked just like the other two girls. But how could that be? The portrait was painted decades ago and she's only 15 or 16. There was only one other possibility… And I had to be sure.

Chapter Thirty-One:
Ryn

Mr. Pete may have been a murderer, but he wasn't a liar. We had the best hot meal I've ever had—meatloaf, brown gravy, real mashed potatoes, and homemade bread with real butter. There was some conversation around the table but mostly about the weather, the hunting season and the conditions of the nearby roads. There was no talk about murder, gold or whatever was going to take place in Tucson. At least not while I was anywhere in the room. It wasn't until after the meal was served when Mr. Pete pulled me aside.

"Tomorrow morning you'll be riding with Hadley, Bill and me to Tucson."

"What about Halloway?"

"We'll be taking a car. Halloway will need to tend to the horses. He has other business. It's a long ride, even by car, so we'll be spending the night in Benson."

"Camping?"

I could see that Mr. Pete was about to laugh, but he managed to keep a straight face.

"No, we have…friends in Benson. We'll be staying with them. You're doing a good job, Rin, keeping your mouth shut. Just make sure it stays that way. Okay?"

"Yeah, sure."

I started to head for the small bedroom where I was going to spend the night when I thought of something.

"If we're taking a car, then I won't need to wear these cowboy boots, will I?"

Again, Mr. Pete looked as if he were holding back a laugh, or a smile at least.

"No, guess not. No rattlers in the big city. Not any that would bite your ankle anyway. So, go ahead, put on those fancy-dancy New York shoes of yours. Halloway will see to it the boots get returned."

Hallelujah. No more tight, binding, cramping, crimping boots. It was one thing to put them on, but no one told me how hard it was to try and get them off. They'd been glued to me for days, sweat and all.

As I sat on the narrow bed, I bent over and tried to pull one of the boots off. No luck. I used the heel of the one boot to put pressure on the other, but that didn't work either. I moved my hand under the heel and gave a tug but all I managed to do was get a cramp in my leg. This went on for at least a half hour and I was getting nowhere. My hands began to hurt and so did my back. No wonder cowboys always said they wanted to "die with their boots on." It was impossible to get them off! I must have been making enough grunting noises that everyone heard me.

Hadley leaned into the doorframe of the room and shook his head.

"Why don't you just use a boot jack?"

"A what?"

"Oh for goodness sakes, I keep forgetting you're from back east. A boot jack. A thing you step on to get the boot off. There's an old wooden one near the front door. Knock yourself out!"

"I spent a half hour in here trying to pull off these stupid boots!"

"Should've asked."

"I don't know what I should ask and what I shouldn't," I grumbled.

"Calm down, you'll figure all of that out soon enough. Miss Ida Mae will have a hot breakfast for us, too. Then we'll be getting in the car and heading to Benson so if I were you, I'd get some sleep. Won't be too hard. Got a real bed this time!"

I tried to remember the last time I slept in a bed. It was back at the hotel in Phoenix. Back in my time, not 1930. I'd make a break for it in Tucson and find Aeden. Then we'd figure out a way back. I remember reading somewhere that nature likes all things in their own time and place. I just hope it was in a science book and not a comic. Poor Aeden. She must really be a mess by now.

Morning was a blur but at least I was wearing my own comfortable sneaks. Washed. Dressed. Ate. Thought it might be my last meal so I took thirds. Got in the car. I don't even remember if I thanked Miss Ida Mae but I hoped so.

Well, I was right about one thing. The car was a Ford. A green 1929 Ford. Ugly green. I'd see pictures of this model in old car magazines and couldn't imagine what it was like to actually be riding in one. Now I know. Uncomfortable. At least for me in the back seat. I was crammed in next to Bill and the window was small, but it could've been worse. Halloway could have been with us and that would have meant I was stuck in the middle between the two of them. Still, there wasn't much room.

The car seemed to sputter and spit; but I don't think it was on account of Mr. Pete's driving. Or Hadley's. Or Bill's, when they all took turns. And they all took turns adding more oil or adjusting something or other under the hood.

The road seemed to be hard dirt or some sort of pavement with huge boulders on either side, lots of scrub brush and rock ledges. The blue sky seemed to stretch for miles. Nothing in-between. If time were to tip to the present I imagine this same road would be dotted with McDonalds, Motel 6's and tons of gas stations. But all I saw was wide open country. I was just relieved that we had enough gas to make it to Benson.

This time we didn't stay on the outskirts of town. I was ushered into a small white house on 4th Street, which apparently was the center of town. To me, it looked like one of those old movie sets where two guys have a shootout in the middle of the street. An older gentleman was the only person in the house and his conversation with Mr. Pete was brief and to the point.

"I heard about the shooting at Morenci Mine. You got out of there in a hurry."

"Halloway telegraph you?"

"Yeah."

"Left the body for the local authorities."

"Heard you found some information, though."

"Not all of it, but enough to tell me I'm on the right track with Tucson. I need to use the telephone, Lee."

"You know where it is."

Bill and Hadley had taken the car to a gas station so I was the only one in the house, except for Mr. Pete and the guy who must have owned the house. A tall, lean, grey haired man with a long white moustache that curled on either end. Mr. Pete had called him Lee. There was something about the way they spoke that made me think this Lee guy might have been the brains of the operation. I don't know. Maybe it was his height or the way he carried himself, but honestly, the guy made me think of the old time cowboy heroes who saved the day in every western movie I've ever watched. But I knew better.

I stood by the kitchen table, trying to figure out if I should say anything or just wait. As it turned out, I didn't have to decide much longer.

"Heard Pete picked you up in Morenci. Outside the mine."

I nodded and he continued speaking.

"Pete's got some things to take care of in Tucson and it looks like you'll be joining him."

"Looks that way," I said.

"I'm sure he'll put you on a train back home if that's what you want him to do when he ties up things."

Again, I nodded.

"There's some milk, crackers and cheese in the icebox, kid. Help yourself. And you don't need to be so jumpy. Ain't like there's a target on your head!"

"Not yet, anyway," I thought to myself as I opened the door to the small white icebox.

Lee kept talking.

"One of the local girls will be bringing us dinner later. I'm not much of a cook."

"I'll be fine. Thank you."

This time it was Lee who nodded as he left the room. I sat at the table and ate a handful of tasteless crackers and some hard cheese. "Only another day or so, Aeden," I said quietly. "And somehow I'll manage to find you once I get to Tucson."

I could hear my words. I just wished I could have believed them.

Chapter Thirty-Two:
Pete Holm

Pete Holm tore the personal ad from the newspaper and carefully folded it before putting it in his billfold. He knew that at some point he would have to show it to Ryn. But not now. Too much at stake. Even if Ida Mae was downright furious with him.

"You could have just left him at the mine, you know."

"And what? Have him run to the local sheriffs? This is too big an operation to run any risks."

"But using a boy, Pete?"

"I swear Ida, I'll make sure nothing happens to him."

"Make sure you get him home. That's what you need to do."

"I need to take care of this business in Tucson. That's what I need to do. Everything else will fall into place later."

"Do you think he'll make a run for it once you get to Tucson?"

"I doubt it. He's scared out of his wits and I intend to keep it that way."

"Good thing you never had any kids of your own, Pete."

"I signed on for another kind of life. One that doesn't leave much time for family."

"Just make sure to get him back to his."

"You always were a soft touch, Ida. Now quit worrying."

Pete gathered his belongings and gave the word for the men to get into the car. As it coughed and choked, a thick cloud of black dust made its way to the front porch. Ida Mae slammed the door and didn't bother to take another look as the men drove to Benson.

Now Pete was facing another hurdle—Lee. He had worked with Lee for over a decade and had certainly proven himself. Still, Lee considered himself Pete's mentor, or at the very least, his conscience. So it came as no surprise that he was furious that Pete had dragged some kid into their business.

As soon as Pete placed the receiver back on the phone, Lee motioned for him to step outside.

"So you're not going to tell the kid who you are, I take it? Or, who we are, for that matter?"

"It would only mess things up. If he really knew, he'd try to play the hero in this situation and manage to get all of us killed. It's better this way. Besides, no one will suspect a kid like that. He'll be able to poke around in places without calling attention to anyone."

"What about his own safety?"

"Don't worry, I'll have Hadley or Bill tail him if it gets to that."

"So what really happened at the mine?"

"Can't say for sure. The shot went off, the guy was dead and here comes this kid before I could do anything about it. I had to get him the hell out of there. I was lucky enough to grab part of the note. It's the only clue we have."

"So the kid thinks you killed the guy."

"Oh yeah. Kid thinks I'm a murderer all right."

Lee chuckled and shook his head.

"You'll have to tell him the truth at some point. But I trust you, you'll know when."

Pete reached his hand slowly into his pocket and pulled out a brass oval badge with an engraved eagle on the top. The center was round and smooth, and had two letters—U.S., and framing it on top and bottom were the words "Deputy Marshal."

PART TWO:
GOLD

Chapter Thirty-Three:
Walter Lewis

Sweat dripped slowly from Walter Lewis' thin sandy hair as he remained pressed against the rock wall of the mine. His fingers still trembled slightly from absorbing the gun's recoil. It was a clean shot, if you could call it that, killing mine owner Thomas Stuart in just a matter of seconds. But nothing else about it was as neat.

As Walter reached inside Thomas' jacket to grab the note he had come for, he heard a quick rustling sound, and glanced back, not realizing that the note had ripped in half. A kid. Some stinkin' kid was in the mine. And he'd probably seen everything. No sense taking a chance. Especially when the gun had more bullets.

The kid was running deeper into the mine and Walter wasn't about to spook him. All he needed was a clean shot and he'd be off with the note. But the mine was tricky and the little tunnels didn't give the kid up easily. Next thing Walter knew, he heard voices and one of them was all too familiar. That's when he decided to stay in one spot, even if it meant the entire day, before making his exit.

Walter was not about to take any chances. He had come too close. So he waited it out, pressed tight against the walls until the last of the miners had left the other channels for what remained of daylight.

It was dusk when Walter finally started on the road back to Morenci. His buddies would really be furious, but what the heck! They weren't the ones in the mine. They weren't the ones with the loaded gun and the last ditch chance to grab the one note that would lead them to lifelong prosperity. So what if they were angry. A ticket to a hidden gold mine would turn their lives upside down.

"Almost home," Walter thought to himself, "with my new road map."

It wasn't until he met up with his younger brother Vernon, and their cousin Merle, that he actually took the time to look at the note. They were sitting in the small room that Merle had rented for the week, having told the landlord that they intended to get jobs at the mine.

Walter pulled a string from overhead and illuminated the room with the light from a small incandescent bulb before unfolding the paper. He took one split second look and groaned.

"Son of a gun! Darn thing got ripped in two!"

"What does it say?" Vernon said, trying to conceal the edginess in his voice.

"It's got a longitude line, four digits and the start of a sentence."

Without wasting a minute, Vernon grabbed the paper and read it out loud before adding his own commentary.

32° 13' 18" N
16-18-9-19--
Helene and

"Okay, so we've got a longitude line that probably runs straight down Arizona and four numbers with dashes in-between. Means it's a combination to a safe and we're just missing one number."

"What about the name?" Merle asked.

"Could be more than one name," Merle replied. "It says *and*."

Walter stepped in front of the men and grabbed the note.

"Look, we know the rumors were all about Tucson, so I'd be willing to bet anything that it falls on that longitude line. But we really need to figure out who this Helene is, because she'll be able to lead us right to the safe. Forget the other names. If there were other names. Doesn't matter. All we need is one and we have it."

"So now what?"

Vernon was clearly irritated and in no mood for games.

"We send a little telegraph to a friend of mine who just happens to work in the assayer's office down in Tucson. If the name Helene means anything, he'll know."

"If it's Tucson we're after," Merle said, "then we'd better get going. We can't afford to sit around and wait for some answer to your telegraph."

Walter took a slow breath, cracked his knuckles and sat down.

"We'll send the telegraph to Tucson and ask for the reply to be sent to Safford. We should make it there in a day if the car doesn't break down. Everyone okay with that?"

Silence.

"Then we all agree. I send a telegraph and we head out for Safford. From there we'll drive south, just east of Wilcox. No sense spending anytime in Wilcox. If someone's on our trail, they might take a back road. That leaves out Benson, too. There's a small telegraph office in Pantano. I'll let my acquaintance in Tucson know that if anything comes up, he's to send a message for us to that office."

"Sounds like you had a lot of time to think things out, Walter," Merle said as he shut the light.

"Yeah, a whole stinkin' day in a dark mine. So this better be worth it."

Chapter Thirty-Four:
Aeden

*I*t was dark by the time we walked home and the only thing we had to eat were some crackers and the two apples we had purchased from a street vendor earlier in the day. My stomach was grumbling and Sue could see how miserable I felt.

"Tomorrow's another day, Aeden. Tell you what. We'll buy our breakfast from the bakery downstairs. Hot rolls. Pastries. You name it. With an early start, we'll really have time to check the house out. Every last inch of it!"

"We don't even know what we're looking for, or if it's still there for that matter."

"Oh, it's there all right. That mine owner got shot because he had some information. I bet there's lots more gold where the first stash came from."

"You actually think we're going to find a vault full of gold?"

"If not the gold itself, then information telling us where it is. You heard the assayer. The sample was really pure. Not the kind of stuff they're used to seeing. That's why he wanted to know where the mine was."

I sighed and sat down on my bed. No use trying to talk Sue out of anything. Then I remembered that we bought a copy of the newspaper with the article about the dead mine owner.

"Sue, where did you put that newspaper? Maybe the article could give us more information."

"It's on top of the dresser."

I looked at the headline once again.

MINE OWNER MURDERED IN MORENCI. SHERIFF'S INVESTIGATION TURNS STATEWIDE.

Then I read the article word by word, trying to make sense of the situation that we had gotten ourselves into.

"Well, what does it say? Anything about another mine?"

"No, Sue. Just that they called the U.S. Marshals into the investigation. The mine owner was a guy named Thomas Stuart. He inherited Morenci Mine from his grandfather, the late Thomas Pearsall. That's all it says. The foreman is going to oversee the operation until the state decides what to do. Thomas Stuart wasn't married and there are no beneficiaries. It doesn't say much else."

"That's good. That means they don't know anything about any missing sock full of gold."

"Well if they do, they're not likely to broadcast it, are they? I mean, maybe the U.S. Marshals and the sheriffs know all about the gold. For that matter, maybe they're looking for us!"

"Oh for heaven sakes, stop it! No one is looking for us. Now put the paper away and let's get some sleep."

I was about to fold the paper in half when I decided to see what else was inside.

Progress on building the Boulder Dam, new radio drama called "The Shadow" attracting large audiences, Her Royal Highness, The Princess Margaret, is born in England, Fox Tucson Theater doing well since it opened on April 11, 1930 and some recipes, a weather report and lonely hearts column.

Nothing at all about a search for two would-be gold thieves.

There was just one page left and I flipped it over quickly. That's when I all about lost my breath and started to hyperventilate.

"Aeden, what's the matter? Aeden, calm down."

I couldn't talk. I just kept gasping.

"Aeden, you're scaring me. Let me get you some water."

Sue went over to our small sink and came back with a glass of lukewarm water.

"Drink it."

I caught my breath and pushed it aside.

"The photo, Sue. The photograph. Take a look at the picture."

Sue held the paper up and scanned it.

"It's a picture of the orphan train, Aeden. The boys' section. They're either leaning out of the windows or lining up for their new families. So?"

I was slow and deliberate with my answer because just saying the words made every inch of my body tremble.

"The third boy on the right is Ryn. It's my brother. In Arizona. Now. 1930. Like me."

Chapter Thirty-Five:
Ryn

The crackers were possibly the worst I had ever eaten in my entire life. Bland, tasteless and maybe even stale. Still, it was food. I hoped that whoever was bringing us dinner could at least cook half as well as Ida Mae. As I finished choking down the last bit of crumbs, I heard the clack of the phone receiver and knew that Mr. Pete had finished his call. I took a breath and waited to see if I could overhear any part of the conversation between him and Lee in the next room.

It's never good to hear parts of a conversation 'cause you never get it right. But...certain words have a way of making sure you get the idea, and believe me, I got it. Loud and clear.

"Mess things up," "Killed," "Tail him" and "Murderer" were really audible. But the worst was when I heard Lee say, "You'll have to....you'll know when" and I knew then and there that they were going to kill me. It was just a matter of time.

Crap. I had no money, no nothing. My only plan was to get away from them once we got to Tucson and find the nearest sheriff. I figured it was far enough away from Morenci and they would not be sending me back to my foster family from hell. I just needed to come up with a good story and convince someone to help me find Aeden. Meanwhile, I just had to stay alive.

When Bill and Hadley returned with the car, Mr. Pete had me get a bucket of water, some flakey soap stuff and a few rags.

"Might as well earn your keep, Rin. The car is covered in dust."

I was about to tell him that the car will be covered in more red dust by the time we got to Tucson but thought better of it. I didn't need to give him a reason to kill me any sooner.

Washing the car gave me something else to think about other than how and where they were going to shoot me. About the time I was finishing, a girl who looked to be about 18 or 19 showed up with a big basket of fried chicken and some biscuits. She walked past me without saying a word and knocked on the door. A minute or so later, it swung open and she scurried down the steps. Lee was a few feet behind.

"Remember, we'll be expecting the breakfast muffins real early."

"I know. I'll be back as soon as it's sun-up."

As she started to walk away, Lee turned to me and said, "That's my neighbor's daughter. Nice girl. Quiet."

"Uh-huh," I said as I wiped the last of the water from the hood of the car and wondered if she was scared out of her mind that they were going to kill her, too.

Dinner was good. Actually, it was more than good. I've eaten fried chicken before, but usually from a fast-food place. This was nothing like that. If this was going to be my last meal, at least it was a decent one. But as things turned out, it wasn't my last meal. Not yet.

I got to sleep on a small cot in the living room. The guys all had beds in the other rooms. For a while, the radio was on and I could listen to music. Really old music by people I never heard of. Eddie Cantor. Ethel Waters. Al Jolson. Maybe my parents had heard of them, but probably not. Then the news came on and someone turned off the radio. They probably didn't want me to hear that they were on the run, but honestly, I had already figured that out.

Another "Hurry-up and get your butt moving" morning! The girl from next door did bring the muffins, along with butter and jam, but I had to eat too fast to really enjoy them. Again we were all crammed into the car, same as the last ride. Mr. Pete and Lee had their own "secret" conversation a few feet away, before waving good-bye to each other. I did manage to yell "Thank-you" as the car started up, but I'm not sure Lee heard.

The first part of the ride was uneventful. No real conversation and nothing but endless cactus and scrub brush to look at. There was a small gas station in a place called Mescal, our first stop of the day. My arms felt stiff and sore from all the car washing; and sitting in one position really didn't help. I used the five or so minutes we had for a quick pit stop and a chance to stretch my arms and legs. Then it was back to the rear seat and more riding. The car was about as miserable and uncomfortable as a piece of torture equipment. I felt every bump, every sway and every single movement the car made. Didn't they have shocks back then?

The steady "thump-thump" of the wheels on the road had started to make me drowsy when all of a sudden I saw a cloud of dust on the side of the car and Mr. Pete yelled, "Hold on! We're pulling over!" Most cars would screech or scream to a stop. Ours thumped and thudded, kicked and rasped until it finally settled itself on the edge of the road, facing what else but another cactus.

I could see it was a motorcycle. A red motorcycle. And oddly, the style wasn't so far off from what's on the road today. I was so engrossed in checking it out that I didn't pay much attention to the driver, but everyone else did. I ducked down, waiting for them to pull their guns and start shooting. The car doors slammed. The men were outside and I buried my head between the back of the front seats and the floor, waiting for a hail of bullets.

Then someone opened the back door and said, "What on earth are you doing? Lose something down there?" I took a deep breath and stepped out of the car, not knowing what to expect. Three things became clear to me all at once—the bike was a 1928 Red Indian Scout, the rider was Lee from Benson, and no one was interested in killing me. Not then, anyhow. They were hovering around Lee and listening to every word that he said as if the gospel itself was being delivered.

Whatever it was, I knew it wasn't good. Lee had driven that bike at break-neck speed to catch up with Mr. Pete. And whatever information he was about to share could only mean one thing. We were in trouble.

Chapter Thirty-Six:

Aeden

I tried pushing the loose strand of hair out of my eyes and behind my ear but it was too short. Annoyingly short. But then again, everything seemed to annoy me. Even the hot rolls and chocolate muffins from the bakery didn't do much for my mood as we made our way back to the old house on Helene and Mabel Pearsall.

Seeing that photo of Ryn and knowing that there wasn't much else I could do, other than run ads in the paper, made me feel miserable and even more homesick. I just kept worrying that I'd never find him.

"You've got to concentrate, Aeden," Sue said as she slid the key into the front door. This time a whole lot easier than the first. "The way you carried on last night about your brother's picture was really weird. I mean, sure, maybe you thought he kept on going to California, that's understandable. But what on earth did you mean by *1930*?"

"Nothing. Just nothing. I was just overwhelmed. That's all. Overwhelmed and upset. I don't know what else I can do."

"You've got ads running. Maybe use a radio ad as well. I'm just afraid of contacting the sheriff."

"I know. A radio ad might work. I read that lots of people are listening to radio shows and maybe Ryn is one of them."

"Only *The Shadow* knows."

"What? What shadow?"

"The radio show. *The Shadow.*"

I suddenly remembered reading about that show in the same newspaper and for the first time, felt a bit of optimism. I figured that if radio was anything like TV or the internet, then everyone would hear the commercials and the ads.

"When we're done here, we need to find a Tucson radio station, okay?"

"Sure, Aeden. Now stop worrying. We've really got to look in every corner of the house for a safe or vault."

"I know."

Sue made sure that the front door was closed and locked from inside before we went any further. I'd have to feign discovery of the cupboard key so I headed immediately to the dining area.

"Might as well pick up where we left off," I said, trying to act nonchalant.

"Open every drawer. Look for keys, notes, anything. I'll be upstairs."

"Do you think they hid money or gold under the mattresses? You always hear about old people dying and having all their money sewn into a mattress."

"I never heard of that, but I'll give a look. I'll yell if I need you to lift anything."

I waited till Sue was at the top of the stairs before going into the dining room. Then, I took out the small key and quietly opened the first fancy side door and sighed. I was staring at five shelves that held fancy serving dishes. And nothing was in any of the bowls. Why they would keep it locked up was beyond me. I moved the small dresser to the other side and unlocked that door. Again, disappointment. More shelves with fancy tableware.

I plopped the key back in its original spot and decided to look elsewhere. Elsewhere and everywhere and still nothing. My hair was becoming sticky from the heat and I tried to remember the last time I had actually washed it. It wasn't as if we had all the modern conveniences at our disposal.

While Sue was upstairs, I overturned sofa cushions, chair cushions and anything that could be moved. I looked in corners, crevices and every drawer I could find in the kitchen, not that I expected a safe to pop up in one of those unlikely places, but maybe a note, or another key or something... After what seemed like hours, I yelled up the stairs.

"Well, did you find anything? Because there's nothing here. Nothing. Unless you want to count the dust."

"I don't get it, Aeden," Sue said as she walked down the narrow staircase, pausing occasionally to touch the banister and look around. "I just don't get it."

Then, like some sort of weird specter, she brushed past me and walked into each of the downstairs rooms, eyeballing everything in sight. I sat in one of the dining room chairs and watched. I could see she was counting the windows, but I had no idea why. Before I could ask, she raced through the downstairs again, this time counting out loud until she finally spoke.

"Aeden! Remember the other day when we walked all around the outside of the house?"

"Yeah…"

"We could see glass panes in all of the windows. All but one. That one had sealed shutters on it. Do you see any sealed shutters anywhere?"

I stopped and thought about it before speaking.

"No, I don't. Oh my gosh. Are you thinking that something got boarded up and the safe is in there?"

"Why else would the window be sealed from the outside, but not seen in the inside? That's got to be it!"

The back door crashed open and Sue was in the yard before I could even catch up. I stood by the doorframe and waited.

"So? Where's the missing window?"

"Just past the kitchen, in the dining room. Hurry up!"

Two vertical windows framed either side of the enormous sideboard, but on close inspection, I could see that they weren't symmetrical.

"I bet the window is behind this sideboard," I announced.

The gigantic piece of furniture was pressed fast against the wall and it would take Hercules himself to move it. Sue put her hand by the back of the sideboard, where it touched the wall, and groaned.

"There's no way to see if there's anything back here. But maybe…Maybe something opens up from inside."

I had to come clean so I told her about the key but left off the part that I had discovered it yesterday. No sense making things worse.

"So you found a little key in one of the bowls and opened the side doors?"

"I did. And there's nothing there. Honestly. Watch."

I dragged the small dresser back to the large sideboard and climbed up while Sue watched. The little key moved effortlessly into the tiny latch and I pulled the door open.

"See? Just more bowls and trays."

"Try the other side."

Again, the key slid inside the mechanism without any trouble.

"More bowls and trays, Sue. Just bowls and trays."

Sue tilted her head and took a step back. Her mouth opened slowly but nothing came out. She just stood there looking at the open hutch until her words could catch up with what her mind had just processed.

"The shelves, Aeden. The shelves. One side is really deep but the other isn't. Step over here and see for yourself. There's something behind the first panel on the sideboard. The back of it has to be a false door. I think we've found it!"

She was right. I could see clearly that one side had shelves that were about a foot and a half deep but the other side only had shelves that were a foot deep and that was only in the center part of the cabinet. Not so easy to recognize, especially in dim lighting like last night.

"Let me take a better look," Sue said as she stood on the dresser and leaned into the hutch.

At first I thought the creaking sound was coming from the dresser but I was wrong.

"Shh...do you hear that? Sounds like it's coming from the kitchen."

"Oh no. We didn't lock the back door. In fact, we didn't even close it."

It was a slow creak, like someone opening a door carefully. We held our breath and stood still. It was too late to do anything else.

Chapter Thirty-Seven:
Walter Lewis

Walter Lewis shook the dust out of his hair and walked into the small telegraph office in Pantano while Vernon and Merle waited in the car. They'd been lucky so far. No major breakdowns and no one on their trail.

"Name's Lewis. Walter Lewis. Friend of mine from Tucson might be sending me or my brother Vernon a telegram."

The man behind the counter turned away and reached for some papers.

"Vernon Lewis. Got a telegram for Vernon Lewis but only he can pick it up."

Walter was about to explode with a litany of curses but decided it wasn't worth the trouble. He stepped outside and motioned to the car.

"Get your butt in here, Vernon. Telegram for you."

The men waited until they were all in the car before reading it, even though the man in the office asked if they wanted to send a reply. Walter shook his head and gave Vernon a nudge as they stepped out the door.

Now back in the car, he tore the envelope from his brother's hand, ripped it open and read it out loud.

FORGET NOTE —(STOP)—
TWO GIRLS HAVE YOUR GOLD—(STOP)—
JAKE SMITH

"Well, well," Walter chuckled as he folded the telegram and put it in his pocket. "Guess it's good to have friends who hang out in the assayer's office. Appears some girls have the gold. This shouldn't be too hard after all. Once we find them, they'll take us right to the money. And guess what? We already know one of their names. It's Helene. Guess that half of a note was worth something after all. Now you don't suppose this Jake Smith friend of yours is going to act on his own without us, do you?"

Vernon cleared his throat.

"Not likely. Why else would he telegraph us? Besides, he'll need backup if he runs into anything."

Walter thought for a moment before starting the car.

"Think I'll send a reply after all."

He stepped back into the telegraph office while Vernon lit a cigarette and blew lazy smoke in the air before handing his pack of matches to Merle.

It was only a matter of minutes before Walter returned.

"So what did you tell Jake?" Vernon asked.

"I kept it real simple. I just hope he doesn't get too greedy."

The telegraph operator collected the fee and wired the response while Walter stood and watched.

ARRIVING TUC TOMORROW—(STOP)—
KEEP HELENE COMPANY—(STOP)—
                    LEWIS BROTHERS

"Is there anything else?"

Something about Walter Lewis made the man uneasy but he hid it well and just nodded when Walter replied, "No, nothing."

Then he watched from the office window as Walter started the engine and drove off, scattering bits of dust and rock in the air. When he was sure the car was a good distance from the telegraph office, he picked up the phone and placed a call.

"Lee Elliott, please. U.S. Marshal's Office in Benson."

Chapter Thirty-Eight:
Aeden

Maybe it was a loose hinge or a hot, dry gust of wind, but we heard the door swing open. We just didn't hear anything else except our own breathing. Sue and I looked at each other and stayed still as statues, waiting for the sound of footsteps, voices, or anything that would indicate someone had entered the house. There was no place to hide in the immediate vicinity. And even if we tried to tip-toe upstairs or head for the front door, we would be found out.

I took slow, deep breaths, trying to exhale lightly, while Sue just seemed to exist timelessly in that moment, without breathing at all. Minutes passed and still nothing. Whatever it was, or whoever it was, did not venture inside.

"I don't think it was anything, Aeden. The door just didn't latch, that's all."

Sue walked out of the dining room, across a small foyer and into the kitchen. I still stood in the same spot, paralyzed by my own fear. It was only when I heard her voice that I stopped shaking and walked into the kitchen.

"Relax, Aeden. There's no one here. I already closed and locked the door so let's go back to the sideboard and figure out how to open the false door."

The wood panel looked solid with no way to open it. We tried pushing on it, pounding it and even banging the adjacent sides. It wouldn't budge.

"Are you sure this is a false door?" I asked.

"It has to be. The shelves aren't even and there's no logical explanation for the fact that the shutters are sealed from within. We just have to figure this out. Maybe there's a teeny-tiny hole someplace. Big enough for a pin or needle. And maybe that will unlock it."

"Okay. But how are we going to find some small hole if we can't even see it? If it's that tiny we wouldn't even be able to feel it with our fingers."

"No, but with paper pushed against the edge, we'd be able to feel for an indentation. It would be a weak spot in the paper. Aeden, was there any paper on the corner dresser or...? Never mind. I almost forgot. There was some really thin writing paper on a desk upstairs. I'll be right back."

I watched Sue take the steps two at a time and return within seconds holding a piece of transparent paper.

"Let's give it a try. Hold the paper steady and I'll move my index finger along the edge of the shelf."

I let out a slow breath and humored Sue. My hand was flat against the paper as she worked her finger along the lip edge.

"I found something Aeden. I found something. Now all we need is a pin or needle."

"There's an old calendar on the wall in the kitchen. And it's hanging by a thumbtack. That should work!"

The thumbtack didn't look anything like the kind I've used, but it was still a tack. A metal tack with a thin tip. I loosened it from the wall, letting the calendar drop to the floor. Then I quickly put the calendar next to the sink and carried the tack back to the dining room, making sure I didn't drop it.

"Here you go."

"Swell."

I held my breath as Sue took her finger off the paper, letting it slip to the lower shelf before pushing the tack into the tiny hole. It was instantaneous. The back wall flipped up, revealing another compartment.

"Hallelujah! We found it! We found it!"

There was a space all right, but no safe and no vault.

"I can't believe it. There's nothing here. What a gyp!"

"You didn't really expect to find a safe full of gold, did you?"

"As a matter of fact, I did," Sue said, still moving her hand around the empty space inside the hutch." "I expected to find gold, or a map or...."

And then she suddenly got quiet. Her face took on an odd expression, almost a delayed reaction to whatever had caught her off guard.

"What? What's going on?"

"There is something here, Aeden. Something after all."

"Well? What?"

"It's some sort of paper and it seems to be stuck to the bottom of the shelf. I'm going to try to get it unstuck without ripping it. I'll just keep moving it slowly, bit by bit till it loosens."

When Sue finally had wedged her "treasure" from the sideboard and pushed it back to its original position, I could see the disappointment immediately on her face.

"It's just an old photograph," she sighed as she handed it to me and sat down in the nearest chair.

"It's the two girls from the foyer portrait, Sue, and at least one mystery is solved. Their names are on the back—Helene and Mabel. Someone also wrote the date when the pictures were taken and some sort of strange poem."

Helene and Mabel, 1868
Two in the spring, noon in the summer,
Three more for the fall, nothing for winter at all.
But if in the summer, you chance upon one,
Time will have moved. All will be un-done.

Sue read the poem out loud and shrugged.

"Lucky them. Someone dated a photograph and named a street after them. But why would they write that poem on the picture? I mean, I could understand the date, but a poem? Who writes poems on pictures? That doesn't make any sense."

"Maybe the poem is about them."

Sue took another look at the photograph and pointed to the bottom edge of the front side. The ink had faded a bit but it was still legible.

16-18-9-19-13

"Same combination numbers. But to what? Where? We've gone through everything in this house."

I didn't know if Sue was angry, disappointed or annoyed. She just stood there, moving the photo back and forth in her hand as if she expected it to come to life or something.

"Why would someone go to all this trouble just to hide a photograph?"

I shook my head.

"I have no idea, Sue. What were those numbers again?"

"16-18-9-19-13."

I could feel my heart beating faster and my mouth opening wide. Like a flash of recognition, I knew what this was, and the one thing it wasn't, was a combination.

"None of them go past 26. The number of letters in the alphabet. It's a puzzle, not a combination to a safe. Each number represents a letter. We used to play these games when I was in..." I was about to say "Girl Scouts" when

I caught myself. "Match up each number to its corresponding letter in the alphabet and we'll have a word. A clue."

"A, B, C, D, E, F, G... oh for heaven sakes, can't we find anything to write with? Where did that piece of transparent paper go?"

"Just keep counting."

"16" was P, "18" was R, and by the time we finished, we had our word – PRISM. And suddenly, everything started to make sense. But before we could utter another word, both of us heard a rattling on the back door. This time it wasn't the wind. And it certainly wasn't a loose hinge. Sue put her index finger over her lips to warn me to keep still. I wasn't about to say a word. I was too busy trying to keep myself from shaking.

We ducked under the dining room table and waited it out.

"We need to get out of here now," I whispered.

"I know," Sue replied. "Let's just give it another minute or two before we go out the back door."

No wonder I hated playing "hide and seek" when I was a kid. The fear of being caught wasn't half as bad as the fear of being surprised.

We crawled out from under the table slowly and tip-toed to the back door, stopping only once to look out the kitchen window. It was safe. It was clear. No one was around.

As we closed the door behind us and started to leave the house, Sue turned, grabbed my arm and pointed to the ground next to the bottom step by the back door.

"Oh my god, Aeden. It's a cigarette butt."

"There's tons of litter and probably more cigarette butts all over the place."

"Maybe so, but this one is still smoking…"

Chapter Thirty-Nine:

Ryn

We were in trouble all right, but it wasn't anything that Lee had said. About an hour or so after the conversation between him and Mr. Pete, strong winds began to kick up and blow. I thought the car was going to roll over into a ditch or something. We had just passed a place called Pantano when the gusts started and Mr. Pete turned his head around and spoke. I wanted to yell, "Eyes on the road!" but I figured he already knew that and decided otherwise. At least for a second.

"We need to wait this one out. I'm pulling off the road."

"Yeah," Hadley replied. "Looks like a real dust devil to me."

In the two or three seconds it took for the car to leave the road and come to a full stop dust came out of nowhere and blanketed us as if it were Christmas morning at the North Pole. Only I wasn't with Santa and his reindeer.

I'd never seen a dust storm before. It was like a winter whiteout without the freezing cold. At least I was glad of one thing. Aeden wasn't in the car with us. She'd be screaming and crying and carrying on.

"Hope no one plows into us," Bill remarked to Mr. Pete.

"I think we're far enough off the road. Besides, there wasn't much traffic. Shouldn't be too much longer. These things usually pass soon enough."

As I looked out the side window I could see that the massive amount of dust made it look as if a total eclipse was taking place. Everything had turned dark.

There was nothing we could do but wait as the dust continued to blow all around us. And, to make matters worse, it even managed to seep into the car, making my eyes tear and my throat hurt. Coughing only made it worse.

"Hang on, kid," Hadley said. "It's only dust and it shouldn't..."

But before he could finish his sentence, big, heavy drops of rain started to pelt the car and didn't stop for the longest time. The dust was gone, replaced by water rolling down every window and getting into every crevice the car had. By the time we were back on the road, the highway had turned to mud and we trudged our way into Tucson.

It was as if the stupid rainstorm latched onto our car and followed us all the way there. Mr. Pete just grumbled to himself and no one said anything. I could see that the streets were flooded and the place looked deserted. But there were big buildings, office fronts and official looking places like schools or county courthouses. It felt good to actually see a big city, even if it was decades and decades ago in the past.

Then he pulled the car in front of a three story brick hotel, left the engine running and got out, but not before turning to Bill and speaking.

"We're at The Congress. Get checked in to our usual rooms. I've got some business to take care of. Go ahead and order food without me. I'll get something when I get back. And hand me that jacket. It's pouring out here."

"Well, you heard him," Bill said to Hadley as he watched Mr. Pete head down the street. "Better check us in while I park the car."

Then, turning to me he said, "If anyone asks you anything, you just tell them we're here to see a man about a horse. Understand?"

I nodded. A horse. *Seeing a man about a horse.* How the heck was I supposed to know what that really meant? And besides, I didn't expect anyone to ask me anything. But there were plenty of things that I wanted to ask. Like where are the exits? Where is the nearest sheriff's office? And who the hell are these guys anyway?

One thing for sure. They knew what they were doing, even if I didn't. And I knew the name for it – Organized Crime.

Chapter Forty:
Aeden

I didn't think we could run that fast, but we did. All the way back to our little room above the bakery. We didn't even stop to look around until we got to our street. Whoever had been watching us either didn't bother to follow us or was blocks behind us. It didn't matter. We locked our door and pushed a chair in front of it.

Sue kept taking deep breaths while I tried to swallow. It seemed like forever before either of us managed to say anything.

"Do you think they're waiting outside?" I whispered.

"You don't have to whisper, Aeden. They can't hear us. And no, I think they're gone. But that explains the noise we heard earlier. Someone was at the back door."

"Police?"

"The police don't go snooping around back doors and leaving lit cigarette butts. They'd knock on the front door first and yell. No, the more I think about it, the more I think we're not being followed. It was probably someone who decided to break-in and steal something. The house has been vacant for a while. And when they heard us, they probably got scared and took off, dropping the cigarette butt."

"I hope you're right. Do you still have the photograph? We took off in such a hurry."

"Of course I do. It's our only clue. The word PRISM."

Just hearing that word made me shudder. If it weren't for great Auntie Zanne's prisms, I wouldn't be in this predicament. But I couldn't let on.

"Remember when we first entered the house and I mentioned that the two girls in the portrait looked as if they were alive and you said something about refracted light?"

"Yeah, so?"

"What did you mean?"

"The sunlight came through the window, hit the prism on the chandelier and the beam of light was cast on the portrait, making it look as if it was real. Again, so what?"

"So I think that's what this is all about. And the poem tells us the time because the sun will hit that portrait in the exact spot at different times in different seasons. It's summer. At one o'clock, I bet the sun is going to bounce off the chandelier and point to something in the portrait. And whatever that something is, will be our clue. THAT'S IT! That's why someone went through so much trouble to hide the photograph, not to mention write that poem."

"Aeden, I could just hug you! What time is it? I'm running downstairs to the bakery. They have a clock on the wall!"

Before I could say anything, Sue bolted out the door and ran down the narrow stairwell that opened onto the street and adjacent to the bakery. Meanwhile, I just sat on my bed staring at the photograph. It was the same girls all right. A bit older. Maybe 10 or 12 years old. Their long curls and cutesy ribbons from the portrait were gone, replaced by rather stark hairdos with bangs.

The girls were standing in front of the house in the photograph. One of them was leaning on the wrought iron fence and the other one holding her hand. Other than the fence and the house, there was nothing else in the photograph that stood out, unlike the portrait in the foyer.

I tried to remember the details from the portrait, breaking them down bit by bit. The girls were standing in front of the large fireplace and there was an oval painting off to one side, just above a red armchair. The fireplace mantle had boughs of greenery that surrounded the old clock, and some tall, white candles in bronze holders, but nothing was lit. "Must have been a holiday portrait," I thought to myself. "But what was the clue?" I knew Sue would be charging through the door at any second and if it was a least an hour or so before noon, she'd drag me back to the house. "Please be after noon," I muttered. "I'm exhausted."

"No sense rushing," came a familiar voice from the hallway. Sue entered our apartment carrying a loaf of bread and a small glass container of butter. "It's 12:40. Didn't realize we'd been at that house so long. I bought us lunch. Don't know about you, but I'm famished. Besides, we'd never make it back by one o'clock anyway. Might as well wait till tomorrow morning and as soon as it's daylight, head over there."

She tore off a chunk of bread and handed the loaf to me. We were both too hungry to bother getting a knife. Or spreading the butter for that matter.

"Can't waste this. I'm putting it in the icebox."

I nodded as I continued chewing the soft, hot grain bread. When I finally swallowed the last crumb, I spoke.

"Aren't you the least bit worried about who might be following us? Or who was standing by the back door?"

"Like I said, it probably had nothing to do with us. And if it did, then all the more reason to get over there as soon as we can before someone else beats us to it."

I lifted the photograph from the table and took another look.

"What do you suppose happened to Helene and Mabel Pearsall?"

"Happened? Why should anything have happened? The photo is dated 1868. They probably had normal lives and died of old age."

"Wouldn't they have gotten married and had families?"

"Maybe. Or maybe they all died in the influenza outbreak in 1918. Lots of people died then. Remember what the librarian said the other day? The city couldn't locate family. No family. So no one owns the place. I just hope your clue is right, Aeden."

We were so busy talking that I didn't notice it getting dark outside. Too early for nightfall.

"Look out the window, Sue. It's getting really dark."

Just then a swift wind seemed to come out of nowhere and rain began to fall in torrents.

"Monsoon. It's a monsoon! I've read about these. They happen all the time in the southwest in the hot summer months. Lots of wind, lightning and thunder, dust storms and rain! Good thing we're inside, Aeden."

I'd seen rainstorms before in Portland, but nothing like this. It was as if the sky was releasing all of its anger and fury all at once. And it released it all night. So much in fact that the streets were flooded the next day and we couldn't get to Helene and Mabel. We were stuck in our tiny hovel for the next twenty-four hours with nothing to do except clean and wait for the sun to come out. I just hoped that Sue was right and whoever was standing by that back door to the house on Helene and Mabel was just a vagrant looking for money. Vagrants and thieves move on. Still, I couldn't rid myself of the feeling that whoever was outside that back door wouldn't be so patient the next time.

Chapter Forty-One:
Walter Lewis

“It's not my fault we got caught in a damn monsoon,” Walter announced as they reached the first mile marker for Tucson. “So stop your complaining. Streets are a mess and it's still raining. Where'd you say this Jake Smith friend of yours lives, Vernon? I want us to find his house before dark.”

“Somewhere on North Court Avenue and Franklin Street. Got it written down. Give me a second.”

Vernon leaned forward so he could reach the back pocket of his jeans and pull out the tiny slip of paper with Jake Smith's address on it.

"The number is 353 North Court. Take a right at the next corner and keep going. We're not too far."

"Think your buddy would mind some overnight guests?" Merle asked. "It's better than staying at a hotel where someone would be bound to notice us."

"Jake won't mind as long as we divvy up the gold and he gets his fair share. After all, he's the one who found out where it is."

"Yeah, and I'm the one who had to shoot the mine owner in order to get it. So we'll talk about fair share later. Meanwhile, just help me find the place."

Other than giving his brother directions, Vernon said very little and Merle decided not to say anything at all.

Jake's place was easy enough to find. It was the only small green house with chipped paint and some old tire rims leaning against the front porch. A few straggly cactus and river rocks dotted the front yard. As soon as Walter cut the engine Vernon headed to the door and began to knock, yelling to his brother and Merle to stay put.

"Well, well, well," Jake Smith laughed as he opened the door. "Looks like you made it after all."

"I'm not alone. My brother and cousin are waiting in the car."

"I know. I read your telegram."

"Don't suppose we can stay here for the night?"

Jake sighed. "Not the best accommodations but okay, sure. And only one night. I figure we'll get to those girls tomorrow and take back your gold. Or should I say our gold?"

"Yeah, we'll cut you in," Vernon said as he motioned for Walter and Merle to come inside. "So where are these girls?"

"Seems they've got a place over a bakery downtown but they've been pretty busy snooping around some old Victorian house on Helene and Mabel."

"You mean it's a street? Helene and Mabel?"

"Yeah, a street corner."

"Well isn't that something. When I saw the note I thought Helene was the name of one of the girls."

"Not these girls. A street. I don't know who these girls are, but that'll change pretty quickly."

Just then Walter and Merle stepped inside the house and the conversation shifted to food, drink and sleeping quarters. It wasn't until the men ate what leftover food Jake had in the icebox and drank whatever beverages he had, that they resumed talking about the gold.

"So you think these girls stashed gold somewhere in an old house?" Walter asked.

"Hard to say," Jake replied. "They've been coming and going into that house as if it were theirs. Only tomorrow I think we ought to give them a little surprise."

"If you think I'm going to shoot some little girls you can forget it."

"Who said anything about shooting them? We just want to let them know that stealing is wrong and that they need to return our gold."

"A little ironic, don't you think? Considering it's not our gold either."

"No, but it will be."

"So how do you suppose we go about this?"

"Now that there are four of us, it should be pretty easy," Jake continued. "We get to that house real early and wait it out. Once they're inside, two of us block one door and the other two block the back door. There'll be no way out for them. And once we have them, we make them tell us where the gold is."

"Then what? We just let them go? They'll tell the authorities. The sheriff will be on us like stink on a skunk."

"Well, what bright ideas do you have?" Vernon said.

Walter took a deep breath and blew the air out of his mouth slowly as if he were exhaling the smoke from a fine cigar.

"We follow them to the house. Jake knows where they're staying. We park the car behind the place. Then we hide and wait. Once they have the gold, we scare the crap out of them and lay low until they go running out of there. That way no one gets hurt and we get what we came here for in the first place."

"But what if they don't run out?" Merle asked.

"They will when they see a gun waving in their direction. Just don't anyone get stupid. We want to scare them, not kill them. Get it?"

"Yeah, we got it," Jake said. "Let's just hope they don't get stupid."

Chapter Forty-Two:

Ryn

We had two adjoining rooms with single beds, wash basins and towels. That was the extent of it. Mr. Pete and Bill were in one room, Hadley and I in the other. I tried to get some sleep but all I could think about was how they were going to kill me tomorrow. I had no choice. I had to sneak away. It didn't help that I had no money, no valuables and no plan. But the thought of getting shot and being left somewhere in the desert was all the motivation I needed to get the hell out of there.

I waited until I could hear Hadley snoring. Then, I threw on my shirt and pants and took some towels from the rack and rumpled them under the blanket along with the pillow. At a quick glance it looked like someone was still sleeping. *This is good, I kept telling myself. Just grab your shoes and get out!*

The door made a slight noise but not enough to wake Hadley. I was still clutching the shoes as I tip-toed down the stairs. Thank goodness there was a small side door so I didn't have to walk across the lobby and be seen by the desk clerk. It wasn't until I got out on the street that I actually put on my sneaks and tied them.

I expected it to be really dark outside but it wasn't. The combination of a murky grey sky and a few street lights made everything look clear. All I had to do was find the sheriff's office. Then I'd tell them about this gang of murderers who had something awful planned. I'd tell them I was from Oklahoma or maybe even Utah and came here to find work but got separated from my sister. But I knew I couldn't stand around that hotel much longer. I had to get moving, even if I had no idea where I was going. My feet felt light on the sidewalk but the rest of me moved like lead. My muscles were still sore from being glued to that horse. As much as I wanted to run down the street, all I could do was walk. I tried not to think about Mr. Pete and what he would do to me if he caught me.

At first I thought it was my imagination, but the streetlights kept dimming. Then I heard the sound of a car or truck and froze. It was coming my way. Mr. Pete would have no mercy. I ran into the nearest building alcove and stared straight ahead. *He wouldn't shoot me in the middle of the night, would he?* I could see the headlights casting their beams on the street. The car was getting closer. *I'm dead meat. It's over.* No use hiding. I stepped out onto the road and waited. A loud honk and it swerved. It wasn't Mr. Pete. It was a truck. An ice delivery truck with a sign on the side that said, "Desert Company Hygienic Ice." An ice delivery truck with a really angry driver.

"What on earth is the matter with you? Are you trying to get killed?"

"I'm trying not to."

"Doesn't look that way to me."

"Really. Someone wants to kill me. Can you please drive me to the sheriff's office?"

"I'd like to help you, kid, but I've got deliveries and the ice is going to melt if I lose time. But there's a bakery nearby and it's probably opening up about now. I'll drop you off and you can ask them for help."

I got into the front seat and watched the sky change color from dismal grey to light pink. It was dawn. With any luck Mr. Pete, Bill and Hadley were still sleeping. The iceman glanced at me and then turned his attention to the street.

"So who's trying to kill you?"

"I'm not sure. Gangsters I think."

"You're not just trying to run away from home because you got a bad report card or lost some money or something?"

"No. These guys are real killers. Honestly."

"Well, kid, I hope the sheriff can help. But he doesn't take kindly to fibs or fibbers. Anyway, the bakery is just up ahead. I'll pull over."

"Thanks," I said as I got out and gave the door a quick thud.

The ice truck had already reached the next street by the time I walked to the small bakery on the corner. I knew the guy didn't believe me, but maybe the sheriff would…

Chapter Forty-Three:
Walter Lewis

"Can't believe there's no coffee in this house," Walter said as he got dressed. "I can't think without my morning coffee."

Jake walked past him and opened the blinds, letting in some light.

"You can get a cup at that bakery downtown. The one downstairs from those girls. If we get moving we can catch them leaving their apartment. Then, all we have to do is follow and they'll take us right to the gold."

"Yeah," Merle said as he buttoned his shirt. "It will be like taking candy from a baby."

"Babies cry," Walter replied. "And they can be real loud. Just remember that. Now what's keeping my brother?"

Jake pushed open the door to the bedroom and gave a yell.

"Get going, Vernon. We haven't got all day!"

By 6:00 A.M. a small line had formed in the bakery. Vernon, Jake and Merle sat down at one of the tables while Walter joined the line. The conversations were short and quick.

"Wheat bread. Sliced."

"Got any sourdough?"

"Two loaves of rye."

"Any day old bread on special?"

Then it was Walter's turn.

"Four cups of black coffee and four corn muffins."

As he waited for his order, he noticed a kid about 13 or 14, sitting at a table, who kept looking outside. Before Walter could count his change, the baker walked over to the kid and spoke.

"The sheriff will be here any minute now. My wife just placed the call."

Walter sat down, leaned into the table and whispered.

"You all hear that? We get our coffee. We drink fast and we get the hell out. Don't need to be seen by a sheriff. Back to our original idea.

We get to that house first and wait.
Understand?"

Vernon nodded.

"What if those girls don't get there right away?"

"Then we'll do some snooping around on our own. Coffee's here. Keep your mouth shut."

Ryn watched as the four men drank their coffee and ate their muffins without saying a word. The line in front of the store seemed to be getting longer.

"Honey wheat?"

"Corn bread. Three loaves."

He was so busy watching the line that he didn't notice the men leaving the bakery. It was 6:35 A.M. and still no sheriff.

"He'll be here, kid," the baker called out. "Coffee's on me. And you can have a slice of day old bread."

"Thanks. I really appreciate it."

Ryn had held hockey pucks that were softer than the bread but he was in no position to complain. The hot coffee had softened it up enough to eat. It was daylight now. Broad daylight and still no sheriff.

"Sorry kid," the baker said. "My wife just got a phone call. Seems the sheriff had an emergency at the Congress Hotel."

Just as the baker turned to help a customer, Vernon Lewis pushed the bakery door open and darted over to Ryn.

"Hey kid. Want to make a quick buck?"

Ryn stared at the young unshaven man who had been sitting just a few feet away from him.

"I don't...I mean...I'm not..."

"Look, kid. It's nothing dangerous or illegal. My buddies and I just need someone as a lookout. Won't take you very long. Easy work for a dollar."

"What am I looking for?"

"My grandfather's will is still in probate and we can't wait for the court to settle it. We need to get some things from his house. All we're asking you to do is let us know if anyone sees us. I mean, it is our house and all."

Ryn stared at the man, unsure of what to do.

"Come on, kid. Tell you what. I'll make it two bucks. Two bucks for a few minutes of your time."

By now the bakery shop had filled with so many people that Ryn could no longer see the front counter. He agreed to go with Vernon before the baker could motion him to stay.

Chapter Forty-Four:
Pete Holm

Pete Holm let out a slow, deliberate breath as he straddled the chair in Hadley's room, leaning his arms over the chair back.

"So you just woke up and the kid was gone, that's it?"

"Never heard a thing, boss. He must have left sometime during the night. Can't really blame him. We scared the living daylights out of him. For all we know he thinks you're John Dillinger traveling incognito."

"Yeah, I might have overdone it, having him believe we're a pack of murderers. I just didn't want him to start playing hero and getting into all sorts of danger, especially where the real killer is concerned."

"So now what?"

"I called the sheriff and he'll be here any minute. We've got to turn this case over to them. Can't afford to lose ground or time tracking down the kid. We need to get over to Helene and Mabel before this Walter Lewis winds up shooting two innocent girls. He and his brother are wanted in Colorado and New Mexico. Lee Elliott was able to piece enough information from the telegraph operator in Pantano to figure out what was really going on. Bill's on his way now with the car."

"Sounds like Walter Lewis' brother had connections in Tucson. The kind that eavesdrop. And when he discovered that two girls were sitting on a stash of pure gold, it was enough to get him moving."

"We have no idea who these girls are. Just that they made one heck of big deposit at the bank and somehow have figured out what Helene really is."

The loud knock on the door startled Pete and Hadley for an instant.

"It's got to be the sheriff," Pete said. "Hopefully he'll be able to find Rin Tin Tin and keep him safe and sound until we're done with our business."

"Then what?"

"Then we tell him the truth and try to help him find his sister. All part of the job."

"You're beginning to like that kid, aren't you?"

"I guess so. Just don't let on when we find him."

Pete Holm opened the door and motioned for the sheriff to come inside. Ten minutes later he had learned all about the Pearsall sisters and the vacant house on Helene and Mabel. Piecing that together with what he knew about Walter Lewis, one thing became painfully clear. If those girls were inside the house, they would never make it out alive.

Chapter Forty-Five:
Aeden

"Aeden, wake up! It's light already. We overslept!"

Sue gave my body a tug and I sat up so quickly that I got tangled in the thin blanket that we had acquired along with other miscellaneous items in our small room above the bakery. I was groggy, but lucid.

"Overslept? We don't have to get to the house until mid-day."

"I know. But we should get there in plenty of time to check out every drawer and closet. For all we know, there may be other clues. Come on, get dressed."

I threw on my pinafore and washed my face in the sink.

"Can't we at least grab something to eat from the bakery? There's nothing up here and besides, I don't think I could work that gas stove."

"Fine. Just hurry up."

As we walked downstairs I could see the back of a kid who looked to be about Ryn's height getting into an old black car. But he didn't walk like Ryn. He moved slower, like his legs hurt or something. I turned away and walked into the bakery. Maybe by now my ads would be all over the place and someone would find my brother.

Sue and I shared a small loaf of raisin bread with milk that tasted like it came directly from the cow. As soon as we were done, we headed out the door and over to Helene and Mabel. The streets were still damp and there were some puddles but most of the water had vanished. With the exception of a few wet spots on the walkway to the front of the house, it was as if the storm never happened.

"Before we open the front door, we'd better check to see that no one broke into the back," Sue said.

"Good idea."

We tried the back door and it was still locked. No windows were broken and everything looked the same. The key slipped effortlessly into the front lock and we made sure to close and lock the door behind us as we stepped inside.

I only walked in about five or six feet when something didn't feel right.

"Sue, I don't how to explain this, but I have a creepy feeling that someone else has been in this house."

"We checked the windows and nothing was broken. The doors were both locked, so it must be your imagination. And look around, nothing seems out of place."

I had to admit she was right, but still, I couldn't help but feel as if we weren't alone.

"Stop daydreaming, Aeden," Sue said. "Let's go upstairs and really poke around. I'm dying to see what's in those bedroom dressers."

"I've never snooped in anyone else's rooms. What if--"

"What if what? It's not as if Helene and Mabel are going to come charging through the door. Now come on!"

A light coat of dust had settled on the lace bedspreads in both of the small bedrooms. They were identical with the exception of the paintings that hung on the walls. Still life fruits and flowers in one room, a landscape painting in the other. We walked into the landscape room first.

"Well, here goes," Sue said as she opened the top drawer of the dresser. "Just old undergarments. Ugh!"

The next few drawers held some yellowing shirts that Sue called "blouses" and a few sweaters. Nothing exciting.

She motioned with her hand and headed to the door.

"Let's try the other room."

The top drawer stuck as if something had wedged it shut. For a minute I thought of my own chest of drawers at home and how they were always getting stuck because I crammed so many clothes into them. I knew what to do immediately.

"Open the next drawer and reach in back. You can pull out whatever is making it stick."

I watched as Sue tugged at something.

"It's an envelope. It must have gotten pushed back in the drawer."

Without wasting a moment, she opened it up and stared at the contents.

"Phooey. It's not a map to a gold mine. Just a letter from one of the sisters. I can see the signature on the bottom."

Sue tossed me the envelope and took a closer look at the letter. There was no return address but the postmark read "New York, 1889." Then she began to read aloud.

November 17, 1889

My dearest Helene,

Forgive me for being so secretive with my whereabouts but I feared that father himself would find out and bring me back to Tucson. I know he never forgave me for marrying Jacob and heading east. But you, dear Helene, can you ever forgive me?

Life hasn't been easy, but it has been mine. I've learned what it means to be independent and self-sufficient. I am working as a bookkeeper for a large manufacturing company. Jacob and I tried for many years to have a child, and finally, we became the proud parents of Lenore. Yes, you are an aunt! My only regret is that I hadn't told you sooner.

Lenore is now 2 years old and is just as precocious as anything. Sadly, my darling Jacob passed last winter from consumption – the white plague. It spread viciously from apartment to apartment in the city.

I learned of father's death from the newspapers. Just a year after his brother,

Uncle Thomas. If only father weren't so controlling, things might have been different. Strange, but I couldn't leave Tucson without taking a small part of him. He probably never noticed but I've carried his gold stick pin with me since the day I left. You know the one I mean, the one with the odd design on the top.

Anyway, I think of you often and will always love you.

> *Take care, my dearest Helene,*
>
> *Your loving sister,*
>
> *Mabel*

Sue had just finished reading the last syllable of Mabel's name when we both heard a loud crash from downstairs.

Neither of us said a word. I clasped my hands together to stop them from shaking and waited for what seemed like an eternity.

Chapter Forty-Six:
Walter Lewis

Vernon Lewis jumped from his hiding spot behind the living room couch when the old mirror crashed to the floor. He was still jittery from watching his brother kill Jake Smith. Jake never stood a chance. Walter was fast and brutal, blindsiding him with the blunt end of a gun as they got out of the car. Then, he and Merle rolled the body off to the side of the house under some heavy brush by a stucco wall. So it wasn't surprising that when the mirror fell, Vernon's whole body began to shake. The nail holding up the mirror had loosened from the wall. Nothing more than that. A consequence of too much desert heat and dry air.

"Holy---"

"Shh," Walter motioned with a finger over his mouth as he had stepped out of the large armoire in the back of the room. "Those girls will be down in a second. Go back and hide."

Vernon was grateful for the quick stretch. His muscles were starting to tighten up from being cramped under the sofa. But he had no choice. He and Walter had been over the plan. It was simple. They were to stay hidden until the girls located whatever gold was in the house. Then, they would make their move. He just hoped Merle wouldn't louse things up. Merle was hiding behind the honeysuckle bushes by the front steps and the kid they picked up was positioned down the street.

The kid was supposed to send a signal to Merle if he saw any sheriff or police cars approaching the corner of Helene and Mabel. Vernon wasn't worried about the kid. He seemed anxious for the money. But Merle? What if Merle wasn't paying attention and missed the signal. Then what?

Vernon crawled back under the couch just as Sue and Aeden came down the stairs. They tip-toed at first until one of them saw what had happened.

"No one's here, Aeden," the girl said. "See for yourself. It's just an old mirror that fell from the wall. I guess the weight of it got to be too much. Come on, let's clean up the glass or we're liable to step on it and get cut. I think there are some brooms in the kitchen closet."

Vernon could hear them traipsing into the kitchen and tried to breath quietly. That mirror had fallen inches from the couch and the last thing he needed was for them to stick the broom underneath that sofa.

From his vantage point, he could see a hand holding a dustpan to the floor.

"Just sweep it in here, Aeden. There's a trash bin just outside the kitchen and we can dump it there."

"Is it almost time for us to follow that light beam from the chandelier?"

Vernon couldn't believe what he was hearing. What were these girls doing? Playing games? And all the while he and his brother thought they were going to lead them to some gold. He was about to get up and confront them directly but he thought better of it. Walter would knock the daylights out of him for changing the plan. So, he kept still and listened.

"The clock on the mantle says eleven-thirty. We've got a few more minutes. Let's go back upstairs and see if there are more letters."

Vernon let out a long, deep breath as the girls headed for the stairs. When he could no longer hear their footsteps, he whispered to Walter.

"They're coming back in a half hour. If they don't lead us to the gold, I say we make them."

Chapter Forty-Seven:
Pete Holm

Bill slid over to the passenger seat as Pete took the wheel. Hadley, already in the backseat, was waving good-bye to the sheriff.

"Hope he finds the kid. If it weren't for the fact that we're dealing with the Lewis brothers, I'd be in the sheriff's car, looking for Rin, too."

"Look, I know," Pete said. "But we need to concentrate on catching Walter Lewis. He's as slippery as they come. We need to trap him and the other two. That's why I couldn't do it alone in Morenci."

The car headed up the road and veered to the right. A few more turns and they were almost at the cross streets of Helene and Mabel.

"I don't believe my eyes!" Pete shouted. "It's Rin Tin Tin himself! Standing against a building as if he's waiting for someone."

"Well, he must have seen something because he just darted behind the building," Hadley replied. "I can get out and go after him. Just pull over."

"We don't have time."

"Pete's right," Bill said as he looked out the window. "Maybe this has something to do with his sister. He may have located her."

Hadley shook his head.

"No, he was standing on that corner for another reason. I just hope we can track him down once we've caught Walter Lewis."

Pete continued driving until the Victorian place was in full view. Then he parked the car a few houses past it. As he put the key in his pocket, he turned to the others.

"We need to split up and surround the house. Hadley, you wait diagonally across from the front porch. Bill, you go around by the neighbors' house on the left until you can get to the back of the Victorian. Understood? I'll approach from the house on the right. Bill and I will be able to look in the windows and see what's going on. The minute I give the signal, he and I break down the back door while Hadley hightails it to the front. Keep your weapons drawn. Don't get sloppy. I just hope whatever that kid is running to, or from, doesn't involve that house. He'd better be anyplace but near this one."

Chapter Forty-Eight:
Ryn

*C*rap! I couldn't believe it. Mr. Pete's car was headed right towards me. I forced my legs to move as fast as they could and ducked behind a stucco wall that separated two houses. Damn cactus! My thighs were still aching from that horse and now I was covered in cactus needles! Worse yet, those men who were in their grandfather's house had no idea that a carload of murderers was headed down their street. And what if that house was Mr. Pete's destination? I had to warn those men.

I kept my body bent over and crept alongside the houses. The old Victorian place was just a few yards to my left. All I had to do was stay low to the ground. Why don't these people ever trim their bushes? If the cactus barbs weren't enough, I got nailed by every lousy twig and branch. I looked down and saw the flat end of a man's shoe. It was shoved into the weeds and groundcover. Geez, don't these people ever clean up? I kept moving until I could see the one guy standing in front of the house. I yelled to him as loud as I could.

"Murderers!"

"What did you say?" Merle yelled back.

Again, I screamed.

"Murderers! Murderers! Their car is on the way."

But before I could finish my sentence and beg the guy to let me into the house, he ran inside, slamming the door. I forced myself up to the front porch and tried the door but it was locked. No sense banging on it. I was sure Mr. Pete would see me. So I crept back behind the stucco wall and waited by the neighbor's house. Even if I had to stay surrounded by dirt and crappy cactus, it was still better than being found out by Mr. Pete.

Chapter Forty-Nine:
Aeden

I knew that the mirror had fallen on its own accord. The plaster just gave way. Still, I couldn't help but feel as if we were being watched. Sue raced into the bedroom and continued looking through the chest of drawers while I kept turning my head to the hallway as if I were expecting some bogeyman to jump out at us.

"There's nothing here, Aeden. Just the one letter and some old clothing."

"What about the nightstand? Did you look there?"

"No, there's only one drawer. Open it."

The scent of dried lavender reached my nostrils before I even found the picture. There were sachets filled with the dried flowers on each corner of the drawer. In the center were some old handkerchiefs. I couldn't imagine having to use those things instead of a Kleenex. But there were a lot of things I couldn't fathom about life in this decade.

I picked up the batch of hand sewn tissues and started to look at the designs when a photo fell out.

"Sue, there's something here," I said. "Take a look. It's a photo of a distinguished looking man sitting in front of that same portrait downstairs. A taller man with a mustache and beard is standing behind him."

"One of them must be their father."

I flipped the photo over and sure enough there were names and a date. I read each name out loud.

Thomas and Herbert Pearsall, 1868

Sue leaned over and took a good look at the name.

"Too bad there's nothing else written on here. I was hoping it might give us another clue."

I flipped the picture around and studied it. The man who was standing looked like an officer from the Civil War. Solid. Stern. But the other man was even more resolute. His expression was serious and austere. I could see that the girls had inherited his wavy dark hair. But there was something else. Something weird. Instead of having his hands folded in front like so many of those formal pictures I'd seen in museums and history books, Herbert Pearsall had one hand clutched to his tie as if he were signaling something. Then, it hit me and I gasped.

"Sue! Your pin. That stick pin you carry with all your stuff in the rag bag, where did you get it?"

"I've always had it. It was the only possession that came from my mother. The orphanage had it with my baby clothes. Why?"

"It may be a coincidence, but take a good look. Herbert Pearsall's thumb is pointing to that exact same pin on his tie."

"I don't believe it! You don't suppose…"

"I don't know. But if it's the same pin, then you must be Mabel's granddaughter. Lenore's daughter. And Thomas Pearsall is your great-great uncle. Or was. I bet they all died. Mabel, too. It's quite possible that since there was no other family that anyone knew of, you got sent to an orphanage. If we really do find gold, then you can use it to hire a detective or a lawyer, or someone who can prove who you really are. All they'd really have to do is take a good look at that portrait."

"I don't know, Aeden, it seems too preposterous. Anyway, it's probably close to noon. We should get downstairs and see where the beam from the prism is pointing."

I put the photo and the handkerchiefs back in the drawer and followed Sue downstairs. Her eyes lingered for a moment or two at the portrait as we entered the large room. The clock on the mantle said 11:53.

"That was close," Sue said, as we stood under the chandelier. "Let's see what those prisms do."

"You know, that chandelier isn't the only thing with prisms on it. Look around. There are at least four small lamps with dangling prisms on them, too."

"Maybe all those prisms work together somehow. We'll know in a just a minute or two."

Beams of sunlight seemed to be all over the room and I really couldn't imagine what was about to happen at one o'clock, but all of a sudden, the beams seemed to combine into one larger beacon and it pointed straight at the portrait of Helene and Mabel.

"Sue, look! It's pointing to the clock on the mantle."

She immediately went over to the mantle, grabbed the clock and flipped it over so she could remove the back panel.

"I don't believe this. This clock is really strange. Usually small screws hold them together and you use a screwdriver or tiny knife to un-do them. But this one is really odd. Some other kind of instrument is needed to open it. Darn!"

Then, without saying another word, she jumped up and ran to the front of the room where she had placed her rag bag when we came in. Sue never went anywhere without that bag and for the first time, I was really glad. I watched as she removed the delicate stick pin.

"Aeden, you may be right," she said as she looked at the decorative design on top. "It's not just a pin, it's a key. This design on the top of the pin unscrews the panel from the clock."

"Now do you believe me?" I said.

"I'm starting to."

Sue's fingers worked quickly as she unscrewed the back panel and put it next to her on a small end table. Sure enough, there was something lodged in the back of the clock, separating the working mechanism from the wooden panel.

I could feel the excitement building in every part of my body.

"Is it a map? A deed? What?"

"A letter, Aeden. It's a letter, addressed to Mabel."

Before I could say another word, she put the clock back on the mantle and started to read the letter.

September 1887, Tucson

My dear daughter Mabel,

I knew you would find this letter someday. You were the only one who could decipher the clues. I trusted the original document to your uncle Thomas, my partner in the Morenci Mines. He must have found you and given you the note. How I missed playing those "Hide and Seek" treasure games with you. Ever since you were a child, you knew how to combine letters and numbers to make your own language.

Can I forgive you for breaking my heart and running off like that? I already have. Life is too brief and too uncertain for one to carry grudges. It has taken me this long to learn that. I am an old man now and I fear that we shall never see each other in this world again. But the next world awaits us.

I have provided well for your sister, Helene. She has been a comfort to me. I pray that when you sleep at night, you will always be cloaked in warmth and love.

To this end, I remain your ever loving father.

Herbert Pearsall

"What a bunch of baloney! I can't believe this. There's no gold, no money, no nothing. What a load of bunk!"

I could see that Sue was infuriated but something told me that there was gold. Or at least money. I grabbed her arm and pointed to the last paragraph in the letter.

"Herbert Pearsall said that Mabel liked to figure out clues. Sue, this whole letter is a clue and I think I know what the next step is."

"What do you mean?"

"Well, Herbert Pearsall used words like *treasure* and *hide and seek*. Then at the end of the letter he talks about being warm and loved when Mabel goes to sleep. I remember that my grandmother used to twist and turn quilts into animals when I was a little kid. Well, I think that whatever treasure or gold there is, Herbert Pearsall hid it in Mabel's quilt."

"Only one way to find out!"

Sue ran from the living room and thundered up the stairs to the first bedroom. She pulled back the bedspread and blinked her eyes from the dust that filled the room.

"Only an old blanket, Aeden. Let's check out the other room."

I was standing in the doorway and immediately spun around and headed to the next room.

"Don't rush in and yank the bedspread back. It'll plaster us with more dust. Let me pull it back slowly."

Sue watched as I grabbed the tip of the bedspread by the pillows and folded it back. Sure enough, there was a quilt underneath. A colorful patchwork quilt that looked as if someone had taken an awful lot of time to sew in all of the squares. I motioned Sue over to the side of the bed.

"Let's pull this off slowly. I don't want to choke to death on the dust."

We folded the bedspread as best as we could and put it on top of the dresser. Then we took a good look at the quilt.

"Looks like a regular quilt to me," Sue said as she reached down to touch it. Then, she moved her hand quickly from square to square. The words came tumbling out of her mouth.

"The squares! Some of them squish! Some crunch! Something is sewn in!"

"Okay, let's not just rip things apart," I said, but before I could offer a suggestion, Sue had taken the small stick pin and ripped the seam from one of the squares. My mouth about hit the floor when I saw what she was holding.

"Treasury notes!" she yelled. "Look! They're from 1869 and other years. And the denominations go from one dollar to $10,000. There must be a least 20 of these and that's just one square in the quilt! I'm trying another. Hold these, Aeden, okay?"

I'd never held a handful of old money before. In fact, I've never held more than twenty dollars. I just kept looking at the money while Sue ripped open another square.

"More treasury notes! We are going to be so rich!"

I started to remind her that the money wasn't ours but then I thought about the stick pin. If it belonged to Sue's mother, then Sue was the legitimate heir to the Pearsall fortune that she was uncovering.

"This square has something different Aeden. I think it's another letter."

It was an envelope all right, addressed to Mabel. But it wasn't a letter.

"Aeden, will you take a look at this?" Sue shrieked. "It's a deed to a mine in Morenci. And it's made out to Mabel Pearsall and surviving children *per stirpes.* That must be some sort of Latin term. We found it! The deed to a gold mine!"

I was about to say something when both of us heard the unmistakable sound of footsteps.

"Shh," Sue said. "Put all the money in my rag bag. I'm tucking the deed in my blouse. Quick! Cover the quilt with the bedspread."

I moved quickly, but not quick enough.

"Not so fast, girlie. Just hand over that deed and I'll be on my way."

Sue and I turned from the bed to see a tall, thin, unshaven man. The stubble on his face left little doubt that he hadn't been acquainted with a razor in a few days. Or maybe he just liked it that way.

"I'm not turning over anything," Sue said.

"Then maybe this will change your mind."

Our eyes locked on the barrel of a pistol, just as a second man entered the room.

Chapter Fifty:
Walter Lewis

Merle nearly knocked the door down as he ran into the house. His voice bellowed all the way up to the staircase landing.

"The kid knows who we are! He called us murderers. By now he's got the sheriff on his way!"

Walter turned his attention and his pistol away from the girls long enough for one of them to grab the bedspread and fill the room with a fine haze of dust, causing Walter to rub his eyes and step back.

Downstairs, Merle was still yelling.

"I tell you, that kid's going to get the cops! We need to get out of here! Walter! Vernon! Where are you?"

Vernon started down the stairs.

"What are you blabbing about, Merle? You were supposed to stay outside."

"That kid came screaming up the block. He called us murderers. For all I know he's on his way to get the sheriff."

"Who's going to get the sheriff?" Walter yelled as he approached the staircase.

Vernon shot a glance at his brother.

"Merle here thinks that kid is going to rat on us."

"For crying out loud! That kid doesn't know anything!"

Then Walter looked at the front door. It was wide open.

"Shut the damn door, Merle or you might as well give every authority in the state an open invitation!"

"What?"

Walter charged down the stairs, shoved Merle out of the way and slammed the door shut. Then, suddenly remembering his real reason for entering the house, he turned and headed back up the stairs.

"Those girls have the ticket to our gold mine and I intend to collect."

Vernon and Merle listened as Walter thundered into each room upstairs, looking for the girls. "Might as well give up, girlies. You're outnumbered."

Chapter Fifty-One:
Aeden

It was the first time I'd ever seen a real gun, and it was pointed straight at my face. Then, in a split second, everything changed. A voice blasted from downstairs and the man with the gun turned away. Long enough for Sue to grab the bedspread and hurl enough dust in the air to suffocate an army. The guy with the gun started to wipe his eyes when someone from downstairs started to yell.

The gunman and his buddy headed to the staircase and I forced myself to take a deep breath.

"Aeden," Sue whispered, "we need to tip-toe behind them and hide quickly behind the couch. It's close enough to the staircase. We can't let ourselves get trapped upstairs."

My body felt heavy and numb. I was petrified, but somehow managed to follow her down the stairs and duck under the couch before the men in the room turned around. They were all yelling at each other about the sheriff and some kid. Then, the man with the gun went running back up the stairs but we could hear him yelling at the other guys.

"Vernon, don't just stand there. Help me search the rooms up here. Those girls are either hiding under a bed or in a closet. Hurry up! And you, Merle, stay downstairs and keep an eye out for anyone who tries to get in the house. And watch that back door. Don't mess things up again!"

I could feel every inch of my body trembling but Sue seemed calm and determined. Both of us were huddled next to each other under the couch and on top of the dusty floor. I tried not to cough, especially when Sue poked me. Her voice was barely audible but I understood every word.

"This is our only chance to get out of here, Aeden. When those men come down the stairs, I'm going to reach out and grab the first one by his ankle. He'll fall and drop the gun. Grab it and point it at them!"

What I really needed was a detailed explanation of the plan and how we were going to escape. And what if the second guy had a gun? Or the big guy who was guarding the downstairs? He probably had a weapon, too. But there wasn't enough time. Before I could even process what Sue was saying, the unshaven man came storming downstairs, using words that would have meant a year's worth of detentions for Ryn and me. Everything else he said was loud and clear. But he never got to finish his sentence.

"Those stinking girls are not upstairs. They must have followed behind us when we____"

Sue edged closer to the stairs and thrust her arm straight out. The guy's foot was close enough to touch and his feet were moving quickly down the stairs. Momentum was on her side. She grabbed his ankle and pulled hard, giving him no time to react. Or me, either, for that matter. It was all so fast.

"NOW, AEDEN!" she yelled.

Sure enough the guy dropped his gun and it landed two or three feet from where I was hiding. My mind started to race and all I could see was the gun. *Please don't let this thing go off when I reach for it. I don't know anything about guns. My parents would kill me if they knew I was holding a gun. These men are going to kill us anyway. Oh my gosh. Please don't let this thing go off.*

Then, I crawled out from under the couch and clutched that gun close to my chest, making sure that the barrel was pointed away from me.

Sue's plan worked. The first guy fell so fast that the other one simply plowed into him on the staircase. They were both trying to get up when something crashed through a window behind us. I froze at the sound of shattering glass and the big thud that followed.

"Aeden! Look out!"

I recognized the voice but couldn't think straight.

Next thing I knew, Sue picked up the heavy glass lamp from the end table and hurled it directly at a man who was coming toward us from the back door. A direct hit. Glass pieces all over the floor and prisms scattered everywhere. The man grabbed his head and stumbled to the ground but not before I heard that voice again.

"Aeden! Aeden!"

Chapter Fifty-Two:
Ryn

My body was really aching from being stuck in that position by the side of the house. It had never ached so badly before, even after track practice. I swore I was never going to set foot near another horse again for the rest of my life. Those men must have had butts made of steel. I had to get up and stretch, and besides, the cactus needles were really starting to cut into me. I leaned forward, pressing the palms of my hands into the ground and gave a slight kick with my back foot so I could stand up. That stupid shoe was in my way. And it was heavy. I turned around to push it aside. Who makes shoes so heavy? Then I took a better look. Words I never used flew out of my mouth like bats leaving a cave. *What the... Holy crap. It's a leg. It's a body. Don't tell me there's a*

dead guy here. I didn't just stand up. I bolted up and looked around. Made it fast. Hell, I didn't want to be the next body. Mr. Pete, Bill and Hadley had either gone inside or were staking the place out from the other side of the house. Did they dump someone here earlier?

I walked as quietly as I could to one of the windows on the side of the house and looked in. The men who were supposed to be checking out their grandfather's house were trying to get up from the floor and a girl was pointing a gun at them. At first I couldn't get a good look at her face but then, all of sudden, I saw her and freaked out. It was Aeden. Aeden. With a gun in her hand and some other girl standing off to the side. Then out of nowhere, the girl picked up a large lamp and started to throw it. I knew Aeden was the target and I had to act fast.

I closed my eyes and jabbed my elbow into the window with enough force to shatter the glass. Then, before I could do anything, Mr. Pete and Bill came out of nowhere from the back of the room and Hadley burst through the front door so hard that I thought it would crack.

"Duck, Aeden," I yelled. "And don't let go of your gun!"

"Ryn? Ryn? Is that really you?"

"These guys are killers. Just keep that gun pointed till I get over to you."

Next thing I knew, Bill grabbed me from the waist before I could get to my sister. The girl with the lamp picked up a heavy piece of glass from the floor and threw it at the big guy from the car. Broken pieces everywhere.

"Let me go!" I yelled. "Let me go!"

"Get under a table, Rin, and stay there!" Bill's voice was so loud that it shook the room.

Aeden had stooped to the ground but still held the gun steady.

"Who are these guys, Ryn?"

"Killers! Murderers! Long story! Don't drop that gun!"

The two thin guys who were on the floor by the staircase were now tangling with Mr. Pete and Hadley while Bill and the heavy set guy were at each other's throats.

"Give me the gun, Aeden," I said as I made my way toward her. "I know just what to do with it."

But I never reached her or the gun. The fight had moved to my direction and blocked me.

Up close, I got a good look at the girl who was in the room with Aeden. She seemed to be a few years older than my sister and was absolutely gorgeous. Under any other circumstance, I would have been tongue-tied.

But I was too busy trying to remove the girl from the back of one of the skinny guys. She was clobbering the daylights out of him as he and Hadley were fighting.

Then, she kicked my shin and I tumbled backwards against the wall. By now, furniture was breaking and the three different fist fights seemed to become one large brawl.

The last thing that I remembered clearly was catching a glimpse at the clock on the mantle. It said 12:37 just as someone jabbed me in the jaw and gave me a shove. I swear it must have been that girl. I felt myself landing on the sofa, or maybe it was a large chair, but when my body touched the surface of whatever it was, everything went blank.

Chapter Fifty-Three:
Pete Holm

Pete nodded as Bill approached the back door.

"I'll be able to see what's going on from this window. When I give the word, charge inside. Hadley will hear the commotion and he knows what to do."

The window sill was eye level, enough for Pete to get a good look. A quick, *act now while we can* look.

"GO!" he yelled to Bill. "I'm right behind you. Darned kid just broke through a window!"

"WHAT?"

"You heard me. Rin just crashed through the window!"

The two men had barely entered the room when Pete caught sight of a young girl holding a gun as if it were a grenade. And the kid? He was busy telling her to point the gun at them.

"Murderers! Killers!" The kid kept screaming. Didn't even stop to catch a breath.

Pete knew it was his own fault for not telling Ryn the truth, but now was no time for explanations. Walter Lewis got up from the base of the staircase and immediately threw a punch at Pete. The force stunned him momentarily but not enough to do any damage. Pete came back with a fist slam of his own that sent Walter stumbling for an instant. And then the two of them were at each other with all the fury and vengeance of old enemies.

Hadley had just charged through the front door when Vernon clipped his shoulder with a quick punch. Hadley was on him like a coyote on a rabbit. Only there was nothing docile about the way Vernon fought. Quick punches, fast scuffling, and spit in the face. Still, it was no match for Hadley's muscle. He gained the upper hand before Vernon had time to react. But not before the older girl decided to topple the odds and jump on Vernon's back.

"Give me the gun," Ryn yelled.

Bill acted fast. He grabbed the kid before the girl could hand over the gun, but not before another girl heaved a giant piece of glass at Merle Lewis. It cut his lower lip and fueled him with enough anger to spark a small war. The battle began as he lunged for Bill, fists flailing.

Walter Lewis pulled back to deliver a final punch to Pete but never got the chance. The Marshal was quick with his foot, wrapping it around Walter's leg and yanking so fast that Walter fell on his back, his head hitting the ground. He tried once to lift himself up but blacked out.

Ryn, still convinced that Pete and his men were killers, grabbed the older girl from behind and started to pull her off of Vernon Lewis. The sting from a carefully aimed foot caught his shin. The pain was so intense that he hardly noticed his back hitting the wall.

It was a quick stumble and Ryn regained his composure. He had to stop the men. And he had to get the gun from his sister. But Hadley, Vernon and that girl were blocking his way.

Ryn moved towards the mantle. His sister was off to the side, just past the fighting. He pressed his body against the dresser and kept moving toward Aeden and the gun. Vernon was using both arms and his legs to keep Hadley from delivering more punches. The older girl had slid toward the spot where Ryn was standing.

He had barely touched her elbow when the full force of her upper cut to his jaw sent him tripping over his own feet and onto the soft cushion of the sofa.

The smaller girl took a step forward, the gun still shaking in her hand.

Chapter Fifty-Four:
Ryn

I must have blacked out for a second. My jaw throbbed. My eyes burned. When I finally could focus, Aeden was standing inches from me, the gun still glued to her hand. I stepped forward.

"Give me that gun, Aeden. I mean it."

"Don't you dare," came a voice from behind me. A voice I recognized.

I didn't turn around. I just propelled myself forward, reaching for the gun. Aeden wouldn't let go. The last time we got into a "tug of war" was over the remote to the TV and Aeden was no match. But something was different this time. She was stronger.

I tried to knock the gun out of her hand by slamming her arm and that's when the feisty girl with the brown hair charged into us. Her fingers just barely reached the weapon. Then, my ears exploded. Everything vibrated. Everything shook. Someone pulled the trigger. Aeden? The girl? It sure as hell wasn't me.

The bullet grazed a large chandelier that was hanging over our heads. Shards of glass were pinging everywhere. I swear the whole darn thing was about to fall on all of us but no one else noticed. Not at first. Not until the gun slipped from Aeden's hand and hit the hardwood floor with a wallop.

I made a dive for it. I could feel the metal against my fingers. Then, it was as if every bone in my hand was about to break. I could see the large cowboy boot that was crushing my hand. The large, thick cowboy boot that belonged to the voice I heard seconds ago. Only now, it was even louder.

"Leave it alone, Rin!"

Mr. Pete had one foot on my hand and the other on some guy's back, pressing him to the ground. The other two men from the car were still brawling with Bill and Hadley.

"Can't you guys do something?" I yelled. "These men are---"

"U.S. MARSHALS! Not murderers. Badge carrying, tax paying, U.S. Marshals. Now leave that blasted gun alone, Rin!"

I couldn't touch the gun if I wanted to. Mr. Pete was still stepping on my hand. Mr. Pete a U.S. Marshal? Was he kidding? I was about to say something when the skinny guy who was locking fists with Bill turned and slammed into Mr. Pete's back. I felt the weight of the boot lifted from my hand but before I could get the gun, the skinny guy was waving it at all of us.

"Nobody move!" he yelled. Then, that girl started to scream. Not one of those horror movie screams or one of those "*Oh my God it's a really big spider*" scream that Aeden's girlfriends seem to do all the time, but a piercing, griping shriek that made the guy's head twitch for just a nano second and that was all it took for everything to change.

Chapter Fifty-Five:
Aeden

I didn't remember pulling the trigger. The blast seemed to come in waves, each one reverberating in my ears. It must have been Ryn. I felt myself letting go of the gun just as he charged into my arm. Then glass starting falling all over the place. Ryn, now on the ground with a U.S. Marshal stepping on his hand. He tells Ryn to leave it alone. But the skinny man didn't. He threw himself at the Marshal and snatched the gun from the floor.

Now it was pointed at me. At all of us. Then it was as if every vocal cord in Sue's mouth let loose. High pitched and loud. The yell came so fast that the man with the gun turned his head to see what she was screaming about. And in that instant, the Marshal reached his hand, grabbed the gun from the guy and threw it clear across the room. It hit the bright tiles that framed the inside of the large fireplace, causing them to split and fall.

The sun had worked its way around the house and one of the beams bounced from the remainder of the chandelier to the fireplace. The glow was startling. As if an actual fire had been set.

The man who called us "girlies" was lying on the floor. Motionless. The skinny guy with the gun tried to run toward the front door but the big guy, the other Marshal, got there first. This time his gun was pointed.

"Give it up, Vernon. It's over."

The skinny guy looked around as if he expected someone to help him. But his other friend, the one who was bleeding from the lip, was too busy fighting with another Marshal. And Ryn kept yelling.

"United States Marshals? You guys are United States Marshals? Why the hell didn't you tell me? I thought you were killers. Murderers. For all I know, you could have given me serious psychological problems!"

The big guy started to laugh as he reached into his pockets and handcuffed the skinny guy.

"Calm down, Rin. The only one who has a problem is Merle Lewis and that's about over now, too."

The guy with the blood on his face didn't have the strength to continue fighting. As he paused to catch a breath, the Marshal he was fighting with gave one final slam to the guy's stomach and he fell over. Next thing I knew, the Marshal who had stepped on my brother's hand was cuffing that guy, too.

It was over. I started to walk towards Ryn. I took two steps and then, the guy who was lying still on the floor wasn't so still. He reached out and grabbed the bottom of my pinafore. I could hear the rip before I fell to the ground.

His arm was tight and strong as he pulled me close to him. But the pressure of a gun barrel as it pressed into my waist was all I could think about.

Chapter Fifty-Six:
Pete Holm

"This gun goes off and the little girlie is history unless you un-cuff my buddies and walk away."

Pete Holm didn't say a word. His eyes moved from Bill to Hadley, glancing once at the floor.

"Understood," he said quietly as he walked over to Vernon. But instead of un-cuffing the man, Pete picked up a small shard of prism that had been lying on the floor. With a quick flick of his finger he caught the sun's beam and hit Walter straight in the eye with a searing shot of light that momentarily blinded him. Enough for Bill and Hadley to make their move.

As Bill twisted Walter's arm, Hadley pulled Aeden away from the man, spinning her around before placing her near the fireplace.

"The tiles!" she yelled. "Take a look. There's gold underneath them. Helene and Mabel must have concealed the family's gold underneath a layer of tile."

"Told you it was here all along," Walter said as he rubbed his arm, still slightly sore from Bill's grip. "Didn't I say there was gold here? Well, I was right!"

"Lot of good it does us now," Vernon replied.

Merle, who was still bent over from the blow to his stomach just stared at his wrists, unable to do anything. When he finally spoke, his voice was coarse and throaty.

"With the Morenci mine owner dead, it would have been ours. We had the note and real proof from the assayer's office. The gold was going to be ours the minute those two girls came to Tucson."

"Sorry to ruin your plans, fellers," Pete said. "But the gold belongs to this estate or the state itself."

Then Sue stepped forward. The edges of her mouth started to form a slight smile.

"Actually, I believe this is my gold. And my house. And I finally know my family name. An orphanage back east will show that I was put up for adoption by Mabel Pearsall's daughter. My mother. The mother who named me Suzanne. An inquiry from the state will prove all of it."

Ryn shook his head as he brushed past Sue and walked directly to Pete.

"United States Marshals? Really? And you couldn't have told me? I could be facing years of counseling to get over this."

"Years of *what*?" Hadley laughed.

The minute hand on the mantle clock moved closer to 1:00 p.m. and so did the sun's beam.

By the time Aeden had taken a few steps to get closer to Ryn the beam targeted the chandelier and started to bounce from prism to prism. No one noticed at first. The light moved faster and faster until a full spectrum of color circled under the ceiling, gathering momentum.

Red Orange Yellow Green Blue Indigo Violet...But this rainbow was different. It had movement. Waves. And Aeden and Ryn were in its path. Both of them transfixed by the light... Both of them oblivious to the intensity of its power...

And then 1:00 p.m. The spectrum of colors turned completely white, obliterating everything in sight for an instant. And an instant was all it took.

Someone, somewhere, was reciting a poem. The words danced in the light until the only sound left was the soft sway of the prisms.

And if in the summer, you chance upon one,
Time will have moved. All will be un-done.

Chapter Fifty-Seven:
Sue

I didn't realize that Aeden had shoved something into the palm of my hand until the light began to spin in circles. Instinctively, I closed my fingers around the object as my eyes watched the dancing display of light and color. Everything else had gotten really, really still.

And then, the beam of light had moved and the room looked the same. The same, except for one thing. Aeden and Ryn were gone.

"Blasted kid," yelled one of the Marshals. "He probably ran out the nearest door with the girl."

"That girl was his sister," I said. "And I don't think they ran anywhere."

"Well, you don't see them here, do you?" he replied. Then, he turned to another Marshal and told him to look outside. I walked over to the door before he did, blocking his way.

"You won't find them. They're gone."

"Do you have any idea where they went?"

"No," I said. "You saw the same thing I did."

"All I saw was the sunlight blinding us from the chandelier prisms and next thing I knew, they left. We'll have the sheriff's office send out an alert. Our office will start looking for them, too."

I watched as the Marshals lead the men that they had captured out the front door and onto the street.

"Can't all fit in the car," one of the Marshals said. "We'll have to haul them to the sheriff's office in two trips. Walter and Vernon will be our first guests. Get them in the back of the car and you two can drive them there. I'll be keeping Merle here, company, until you get back."

"Okay, Pete," one of them answered.

As the men were talking, I slowly opened my hand to see what Aeden had given me. It was a small tube of some sort, but not made of glass or metal. It felt like rubber but it wasn't. It was pliable and clear with a split down the middle. Strange. Aeden had given me a message. I just needed to figure it out.

I was still staring at the small object when the Marshal approached me.

"I don't suppose you can tell me anything about those kids, can you? Or should I say, will you?"

I glanced at the prisms that were still shaking slightly in the chandelier. I couldn't tell him what I really thought. If I had to think of a word or an expression, I imagine it would be *Light Riders.* Because the object I was holding did not come from this time or place. And neither did Aeden nor her brother. I just needed to learn how they did it. But, hey, I've got money now, U.S. Treasury Notes stashed in my shirt. And gold, once I prove my inheritance. I always did like science. And the fall semester will start soon at the university...I slipped the tiny piece of tube into my pocket and looked directly at his face.

"I thought they were orphans like me. Orphans who had a long ride west."

He nodded and glanced at the front door before turning his attention to the man he had just arrested.

I moved closer to the foyer and stopped to take a really good look at the portrait of Helene and Mabel Pearsall. The round, dark eyes, the brown curly hair...It was like looking at my own portrait, if anyone had bothered to paint one of me. And then something caught my eye. Strange, that we hadn't noticed it before. It was subtle. But it was there all right. We just never looked.

Helene's eyes followed the artist, watching every move. But Mabel, well, that's the odd thing. Her eyes were off to the side, staring directly at the prisms in the chandelier. Behind her, the mantle clock read 1:00 p.m. She must have known.

Chapter Fifty-Eight:
Ryn

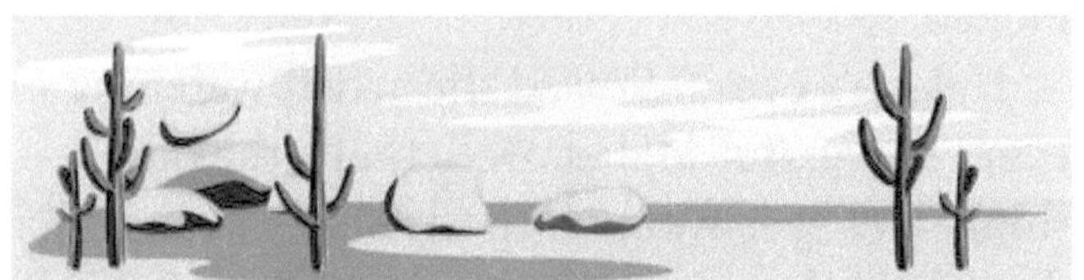

A crack in space. A snap in time. Aeden's face kept flashing in front of me like a strobe light. I felt like heaving my guts out but everything was moving so fast in front of me that I couldn't do anything. Someone or something hit me on the side of my head and I fell. It was forever until my body made contact with the ground. I closed my eyes, waiting for the nausea to pass.

When I could finally stand up, Aeden was lying a few feet away. We were both in Auntie Zanne's yard, next to the small cactus plants. Aeden was still wearing that pinafore of hers but it was all rumpled up and torn. She started to get up slowly as I approached.

"Ryn...Oh my gosh...we're back."

I grabbed her hand and helped her up.

"Why are you walking so funny?" she said.

"You mean why am I in agonizing pain? Because my butt was plastered to the seat of a horse for days on end. And that wasn't the worst part."

And then a voice out of nowhere.

"Ryn! Aeden! Look at both of you! You're filthy. Absolutely filthy! And Aeden, your new pinafore is torn. What on earth have you two been doing?"

I was so busy looking at my sister that I didn't bother to look down or I would have seen that my shirt was covered in dirt and my pants were not much better. My sneakers were caked in red dust and my hair was glued to my head. Aeden and I were probably still struggling to stand up when Mom and Dad pulled up and got out of the car. I had to think fast.

"We're doing what you asked us to do. Clean out Auntie Zanne's junk. We couldn't help it if the stuff was so dirty!"

My mother just shook her head.

"Go inside, both of you. And wash up. Your father and I have some news from the bank. Meanwhile, we're going to take a look around this yard to see what needs to be hauled away."

Once inside I grabbed a towel from the kitchen and turned to Aeden.

"It's like we never left, Aeden. Maybe Auntie Zanne wasn't so crazy after all. The prisms, the gold...it all happened, didn't it? And you're not going to believe what I went through. I was scared out of my mind half the time."

"Well, I got to meet Auntie Zanne, or should I say, Auntie Suzanne. And all of the things we heard were true and a whole lot more. I just wish I knew what happened to her after we left. It was seconds ago and yet…it was years ago, decades ago. That day in the house on Helene and Mabel where we nearly got killed. It was so exciting."

"Exciting? A gun went off near my head. I could be psychologically damaged for life. Lucky I'm not deaf."

"I had a gun aimed at me! Two guns if you count the crazy skinny guy. I should be the one all freaking out by now!"

"What do you suppose happened after we got twisted forward in time?"

"I have no idea. Should we tell Mom and Dad?"

"Are you nuts, Aeden? If we tell them, we'll be spending the next vacation in therapy. So, no! Don't breathe a word of it."

Aeden nodded and wiped her elbows with a dish towel.

"I miss her, Ryn."

"I only got a quick look at her. Boy, she was hot!"

"She was more than pretty, Ryn. She was really smart and amazingly determined. Wish I could have known her better."

"Wish you could have talked her out of collecting crap."

"She had her reasons."

"In a strange sort of way I miss the guys who brought me to Tucson. Hadley most of all. I'll tell you about it someday."

I threw the towel in the sink and walked outside to hear whatever news my folks had from the bank but before I could open the door, Aeden gave me a big hug.

"Most of all, I missed you, Ryn. I missed you!"

"Yeah, me, too. By the way, have you ever heard of a dog named Rin Tin Tin?"

Chapter Fifty-Nine:
Aeden

*I*t all happened so fast that by the time I realized I was staring at Ryn, the shot went off. Then the struggle, the chandelier, the prism lights and Sue yelling. Time ended, or at least took a break. I never got to say good-bye. Next thing I knew we were back in the yard and Mom and Dad were pulling up in the car. My mouth felt mushy and my body even worse.

Ryn was obnoxious as usual, always complaining. But it sure was great to see him again. When both of us finished wiping off most of the dirt and dust, Mom and Dad were waiting for us in the front yard. They were seated on a chipped ceramic patio set. Ryn and I walked over and shared the small white bench. My mother was the first to speak.

"It was a long morning at the bank and I know both of you must be famished. As soon as we finish what we have to say we'll go get a bite to eat. All right?"

We shook our heads and my mother continued.

"First, we have good news. Not only were we named executors of your aunt's trust, but we are the sole beneficiaries of her will. And that's not all."

"What do you mean?" Ryn said.

"What your mother is trying to tell you," my father explained, "is that this house in Wadell is only part of her estate. Apparently she just used it when she had business in Phoenix. There's another home in Tucson and apparently it's quite large. It dates back to the 1800's and was built by her great grandfather, Herbert Pearsall. He was a prominent railroad mogul and financier with all sorts of mining interests."

I gasped.

"No way am I hoeing out that house!" Ryn said, staring right into my dad's eyes.

"Relax, Ryn. I know. It's way too much work for any of us to tackle. But...we'll have the funds to do so."

Then my mother looked at me.

"What's the matter with you, Aeden? You look as if you've seen a ghost."

"I'm fine. Just surprised, that's all."

My dad tapped Ryn on the shoulder and smiled.

"You and your sister deserve a real vacation. So...we'll take one. We'll drive down to Tucson and check out this house. Then, what do you say we spend a week at a dude ranch? It'll be great fun. You can learn how to ride a horse."

It was the first and only time I'd seen my brother lose it. My dad pressed on.

"Well, what do you say?"

"No! No dude ranch! No horses! That's a horrible idea. I'd rather clean a dozen Auntie Zanne houses!"

My dad was flabbergasted.

"What in heaven's name is the matter with you, Ryn? Thought you'd enjoy some relaxation. Guess I'll never understand teenagers."

As he and my mom got up from the table, I started to laugh. Only Ryn didn't think it was very funny.

"You have no idea, Aeden. No idea whatsoever. You didn't have to sit on a smelly horse in tight boots for days on end."

"Serves you right, Ryn," I said. "This was, after all, your idea."

Then I turned and headed to the car, glancing back at my brother. Ryn bent down and started to pick up the prisms one by one.

"Leave them," I yelled. But my brother had already pocketed most of them and was quickly grabbing the remaining ones.

I stood by the rear of the car and waited for him to approach before saying anything else. Then, quietly, I whispered.

"It's all in the refraction, isn't it?"

"No, Aeden. It's what Auntie Zanne did with it."

Then he elbowed me just as I was opening the car door.

"She knew how to bend light, Aeden. And travel with it. And I think she wanted us to figure it out, too."

"But..."

"Don't worry. We'll get it right next time."

-The End-

WORKS CITED

www.goldcalculator.org
www.mining-technology.com/projects/morenci/
www.oldradio.com
www.orphantraindepot.com/
www.pbs.org/wgbh/amex/orphan/
www.scienceworld.wolfram.com/physics/SnellsLaw.html
www.visitTucson.org

Wikipedia Cites:

En.wikipedia.org/wiki/Prism_ (geometry)
En.wikipedia.org/wiki/Greenlee_County_Arizona

ACKNOWLEDGEMENTS

Sincere thanks to my amazing editors (Ellen Beth Lynes, Susan Morrow, Suzanne Scher, Sue Schwartz, Steve Somers, Lisa Tonks) and to my research/technology team (Larry Finkelstein, James Clapp). Your support has been invaluable.

Study Guide for

Light Riders and the Morenci Mine Murder

This young adult adventure novel blends historical and science fiction. The study guide component provides teachers with differentiated questions and activities designed to develop thinking skills and promote a better understanding of this particular era in time. The study guide is reproducible for classroom use.

Chapters One—Five:

1. Do you agree with Aeden that we only see and understand bits and pieces of the people in our lives?
2. What is a hoader?
3. Why do you think people hoard?
4. How do Aeden and Ryn's approach to their task differ?
5. Are you more like Aeden or Ryn? Explain.
6. What do you suppose Auntie Zanne meant when she said, "It's all in the refraction"?

7. What are prisms used for?
8. Is there such a thing as time travel? Explain.

Chapters Six—Ten:

1. Can you explain Snell's Law? If you cannot, ask your science teacher.
2. What was the "Orphan Train"? If you do not know, ask your Social Studies teacher.
3. Explain the Great Depression. What was it? Can you compare it to the economic times we are now facing in the early twenty-first century? (Feel free to make a Venn Diagram).
4. Describe the family that "adopted" Ryn.
5. Why do you think Aeden followed the girl on the train?
6. Would you have taken the same chance as Ryn when he decides to leave the house at night? Explain.

Chapters Eleven—Fifteen:

1. Sue decides to mine for her own gold and says she can always pay back Phelps Dodge. Is this stealing or borrowing? Explain.

2. What do you think motivates Sue? Explain.
3. Was Ryn justified in taking the bike from the porch?
4. What does the term "vein" mean as it is used in this story?
5. Aeden doesn't want to look at the dead body but something compels her to do so. Have you ever tried to look away from something only to be drawn back to it? Explain.
6. Ryn makes the choice to go with the murderer. What would you have done?
7. Why was the rag-bag so important to Sue?
8. Should Sue have taken the gold from the dead man?

Chapters Sixteen—Twenty:

1. Ryn decided to eavesdrop at the cabin. Would you have taken the same risk?
2. Justify Sue's reasons for lying to all of the people on her way to Tucson.
3. How does Sue regard Aeden's education? Is Sue an "academic snob"? Explain.
4. Have you ever read anything by Charles Dickens? (If not, you should!)

5. Do you agree or disagree with the following statement? <u>Sue is resourceful.</u>
6. Have you ever heard of "Rin Tin Tin"?
7. List 5 things you know about President Theodore Roosevelt and President Franklin Delano Roosevelt.
8. Why do you suppose Pete Holm made Ryn figure out how to saddle a horse on his own?

Chapters Twenty-one—Twenty-five:

1. Do you agree with Pete Holm that "a little fear makes for a lot of obedience"? Explain.
2. Pick a small paragraph from this chapter and try to write it in cursive. Can you? Why or why not?
3. Who is "Mrs. Grundy"? What does that 1920's expression mean? (Use Google if you need to find out).
4. Why was Ryn convinced that Pete and his men might be famous murderers?
5. Pick the city you live in and find its longitude and latitude. If Sue and Aeden could do it, so can you!
6. Why does Sue consider Aeden to be "mousey"? Explain.

7. Ryn finds a tick on his chest. What kinds of ticks are found in the southwest? Should Ryn have been concerned?

Chapters Twenty-six—Thirty:

1. What is the secret message in Aeden's newspaper ad?
2. Sue believes in taking chances. Explain her reasoning.
3. How does camping in 1930 compare with today? Use a Venn Diagram for similarities and differences.
4. Why do you think Aeden agrees to enter the house?
5. Do you think Sue knows about the properties of refraction? Explain.
6. Do you think Pete Holm will change his mind about taking Ryn with him?
7. Draw a picture of the house on the corner of Helene and Mabel.

Chapters Thirty-one—Thirty-five:

1. Given Ryn's description, what do you suppose cars were like back in 1930?
2. What is an icebox? What replaced it?
3. Why do you suppose Pete Holm doesn't tell Ryn that he (Pete) is really a U.S. Marshal?

4. Describe Walter Lewis using only 4 – 5 adjectives.
5. Pick one of the events that Sue and Aeden read about in the newspaper and conduct some research of your own regarding that event.
6. What do you think Lee Elliott told Pete and his men?

Chapters Thirty-six—Forty:

1. Do you think Aeden should have told Sue the truth regarding traveling back in time? Why or why not?
2. Why was the radio show *The Shadow* so popular in the 1930s? Do some research!
3. Write a telegram to Pete Holm, telling him that the real murder is on his way to Tucson. Use only 2 – 3 sentences.
4. What do you suppose the poem on the back of the picture means?
5. How are dust storms and whiteouts alike and different?
6. Can you think of a modern expression that means the same thing for "seeing someone about a horse"?

Chapters Forty—Forty-Five:

1. Who do you think was standing at the back door of the house at Helene and Mabel?
2. Do Walter, Vernon, Merle and Jake have a really good plan?
3. Do you think Ryn made the right choice to leave the hotel when he did? Explain.
4. Do you agree with Ryn's choice to go with Vernon? Explain your reasoning.
5. Has your opinion of Pete Holm changed? Why or why not?
6. Mabel had to make a difficult decision. Think of a time in your life when you had to make a tough decision. What did you do and why?

Chapters Forty-six—Fifty:

1. Why do you suppose Jake Smith was killed? What was the motive?
2. If you were Pete Holm, would you have stopped to get Ryn? Explain.
3. What is the one thing that Ryn doesn't see in the bushes by the house? Describe his reaction if he really took a good look.
4. Why is Sue so intent on getting to the beam from the prism?

5. Yes or no. <u>Aeden and Sue are quick thinkers.</u> What evidence do you have to support your decision?

Chapters Fifty-one—Fifty-five:

1. Aeden and Sue take a formidable risk by tip-toeing behind the killers on the staircase. What would you have done? Why?
2. Yes or no. <u>Aeden is brave.</u> Support your answer.
3. What do you think of Pete Holm's tactics?
4. Do you think things would have been different if Pete Holm had told Ryn the truth?

Chapters Fifty-six—Fifty-nine:

1. Why do you think Helene and Mabel Pearsall hid the gold in the fireplace tiles?
2. What do you think happened to Aeden and Ryn at 1:00 p.m.?
3. What do you think Suzanne will do with her life? Explain.
4. If you were Aeden or Ryn would you tell your parents what really happened?

5. Do you think Ryn and Aeden will use the prisms again to travel back in time? Explain.
6. Why didn't the U.S. Marshals read Walter, Vernon and Merle their rights? (Hint: Think 1966)

If you could travel back to any era in time, where would you go? Why?

Thematic Classroom Projects:

- Laws of Refraction (Science)
- Mining Copper and Gold (Science and Social Studies)
- History of the Orphan Trains (Social Studies)
- History of the U.S. Marshal Service (Social Studies)
- Hoarding (Psychology)

ABOUT THE AUTHOR

New York native Ann I. Goldfarb spent most of her life in education, first as a classroom teacher and later as a middle school principal and professional staff developer. Writing has always been an integral part of her world. Her freelance non-fiction can be found in trade magazines for Madavor Media and Jones Publications, but her real passion is writing mystery-suspense for young adult audiences. Time travel is the vehicle she has chosen to embrace.

Ann resides with her family near the foothills of the White Tank Mountains in Arizona.

www.ingramcontent.com/pod-product-compliance
Lightning Source LLC
Chambersburg PA
CBHW051249210726

48287CB00002B/417